THE BILINGUAL SERIES OF
THE MOST IMPRESSIVE BEAUTY OF CHINA

最美中国双语系列

中国故事

CHINESE STORIES

主　编◎青　闰
副主编◎张　雍　宰　倩
参　编◎宋　娟　吕　苗　程留仓

中国科学技术大学出版社

内 容 简 介

"最美中国双语系列"是一套精品文化推广图书,包括《风景名胜》《民俗文化》《饮食文化》《杰出人物》《科技成就》《中国故事》六册,旨在传播中华优秀文化,传承中华民族宝贵的民族精神,展示奋进中的最美中国,可供广大中华文化爱好者、英语学习者及外国友人参考使用。

本书介绍了一些具有代表性的中国民间故事和成语故事,有助于读者从中了解中华优秀传统文化的智慧内涵。

图书在版编目(CIP)数据

中国故事:英汉对照/青闰主编. —合肥:中国科学技术大学出版社, 2021.11

(最美中国双语系列)

ISBN 978-7-312-05231-6

Ⅰ.中… Ⅱ.青… Ⅲ.故事—作品集—中国—英、汉 Ⅳ.I247.81

中国版本图书馆CIP数据核字(2021)第121010号

中国故事
ZHONGGUO GUSHI

出版	中国科学技术大学出版社
	安徽省合肥市金寨路96号,230026
	http://press.ustc.edu.cn
	https://zgkxjsdxcbs.tmall.com
印刷	安徽国文彩印有限公司
发行	中国科学技术大学出版社
经销	全国新华书店
开本	880 mm×1230 mm 1/32
印张	7.625
字数	178千
版次	2021年11月第1版
印次	2021年11月第1次印刷
定价	35.00元

前 言 Preface

文化是一个国家与民族的灵魂。"最美中国双语系列"旨在弘扬和推广中华优秀文化,突出文化鲜活主题,彰显文化核心理念,挖掘文化内在元素,拓展文化宽广视野,为广大读者了解、体验和传播中华文化精髓提供全新的视角。本系列图书秉持全面、凝练、准确、实用、自然、流畅的撰写原则,全方位、多层面、多角度地展现中华文化的源远流长和博大精深,对于全民文化素质的提升具有独特的现实意义,同时也为世界文化的互联互通提供必要的借鉴和可靠的参考。

"最美中国双语系列"包括《风景名胜》《民俗文化》《饮食文化》《杰出人物》《科技成就》《中国故事》六册,每册中的各篇文章以文化剪影为主线,以佳句点睛、情景对话和生词注解为副线,别出心裁,精彩呈现中华文化的方方面面。

"最美中国双语系列"充分体现以读者为中心的编写理念,从文化剪影到生词注解,读者可由简及繁、由繁及精、由精及思地感知中国文化的独特魅力。书中的主线和副线是一体两面的有机结合,不可分割,如果说主线是灵魂,副线则是灵魂的眼睛。

"最美中国双语系列"的推出,是讲好中国故事、展现中国立场、传播中国文化的一道盛宴,读者可以从中感悟生活。

《中国故事》包括民间故事和成语故事两大部分:第一部分有披肝沥胆的盘古开天地、女娲补天、女娲造人、夸父逐日,有感天动地的愚公移山、大禹治水、神农尝百草、花木兰代父从军,有浪漫神奇的嫦娥奔月、牛郎织女、白蛇传、梁山伯与祝英台,还有锲而不舍的后羿射日、精卫填海、钻木取火、仓颉造字;第二部分有精诚所至的三顾茅庐、高山流水、老马识途,有出奇制胜的望梅止渴、围魏救赵、完璧归赵,更有让人警醒的滥竽充数、画蛇添足、掩耳盗铃……可谓精挑细选,精彩无限。

本书由河南泌阳碧水江南实验学校张雍撰写初稿,焦作大学宰倩、人民邮电出版社宋娟撰写二稿,焦作大学吕苗与程留仓撰写三稿,焦作大学青闰负责全书统稿与定稿。

最后,在本书即将付梓之际,衷心感谢中国科学技术大学出版社的大力支持,感谢朋友们的一路陪伴,感谢家人们始终不渝的鼓励和支持。

青 闰

2021年3月6日

目 录 Contents

前言 Preface ··· i

第一部分 民间故事
Part I Folk Tales

盘古开天地 Pangu Created Heaven and Earth ····················003

女娲补天 Nvwa Patched up the Sky ·································008

女娲造人 Nvwa Created Human Beings ·····························013

大禹治水 Yu the Great Combated the Flood ·······················018

神农尝百草 Shennong Tasted Hundreds of Herbs ················023

愚公移山 Foolish Old Man Removed the Mountains ············028

嫦娥奔月 Chang'e Flew to the Moon ································033

后羿射日 Houyi Shot down the Suns ·······························038

夸父追日 Kuafu Chased the Sun ····································043

精卫填海 Jingwei Filled up the Sea ·································048

钻木取火 Drill the Wood to Get Fire ·······························053

仓颉造字 Cangjie Created Chinese Characters ····················058

牛郎织女 Cowherd and Weaving Girl ·······························063

白蛇传 The Legend of White Snake ·································069

梁山伯与祝英台 Liang Shanbo and Zhu Yingtai ················074

花木兰代父从军 Hua Mulan Joined the Army for Her Father ··079

第二部分　成语故事
Part II　Idiom Stories

三顾茅庐	Make Three Calls at the Thatched Cottage	················087
望洋兴叹	Lament One's Littleness before the Vast Ocean	················092
高山流水	High Mountains and Flowing Water	················097
破镜重圆	A Broken Mirror Joined Together	················102
名落孙山	Fall behind Sun Shan	················107
才高八斗	A Person of Great Talent	················112
枕戈待旦	Maintain Combat Readiness	················117
卧薪尝胆	Sleep on the Brushwood and Taste the Gall	················122
沉鱼落雁	Make Fish Sink and Wild Geese Alight	················127
滥竽充数	Make up the Number	················132
画蛇添足	Draw a Snake and Add Feet to It	················137
按图索骥	Look for a Steed by Its Picture	················142
揠苗助长	Uproot Seedlings to Spur Growth	················147
亡羊补牢	Mend the Fold after the Sheep Is Lost	················152
邯郸学步	Imitate to Walk in Handan	················157
讳疾忌医	Hide One's Sickness for Fear of Treatment	················162
掩耳盗铃	Cover the Ears to Steal the Bell	················167

目录

画饼充饥	Draw a Cake to Satisfy Hunger	172
狐假虎威	The Fox Borrows the Tiger's Fierceness	176
老马识途	An Old Horse Knows the Way	181
井底之蛙	A Frog Living at the Bottom of a Well	186
守株待兔	Stay by a Stump to Wait for Hares	190
鹬蚌相争	A Battle Between a Snipe and a Clam	195
完璧归赵	Return the Jade Intact to the State of Zhao	200
围魏救赵	Besiege the State of Wei to Rescue the State of Zhao	205
班门弄斧	Show off One's Skill with an Axe before Lu Ban	210
兔死狗烹	Kill the Hounds for Food Once the Hares Are Bagged	215
望梅止渴	Quench Thirst by Thinking of Plums	220
买椟还珠	Get the Casket and Return the Pearl	225
洛阳纸贵	Paper Is Dear in Luoyang	230

第一部分　民间故事

Part I　Folk Tales

盘古开天地

Pangu Created Heaven and Earth

导入语 Lead-in

盘古是中国古代传说中开天辟地的神,是自然大道的化身。开天辟地的传说寓意深刻、内涵丰富,是研究宇宙起源、创世说和人类起源的重要线索。盘古开天地是中国最美丽的创世传说,讲述了宇宙与万物的最初起源。盘古开天地的故事始记于三国时期徐整所著的《三五历纪》:"天地混沌如鸡子,盘古生其中。万八千岁,天地开辟,阳清为天,阴浊为地……"显然,盘古是中国古人对人类始祖的神化,盘古开天地的传说代表着中华民族关于宇宙起源和人类起源的重要认识,蕴含着天人合一的哲学思想。

文化剪影　Cultural Outline

The **mythology**① of Pangu Created Heaven and Earth was first recorded in the *Three-Five **Chronicle***② in the Period of the Three Kingdoms. After the continuous development and changes, it gradually became rich in content, spread in a wider range and more various forms. And now it has been the most representative mythology of creation in China and of rich cultural **significance**③.

盘古开天地的神话传说始记于三国时期的《三五历纪》,经过不断的发展和演绎,故事内容逐渐丰富,流传范围逐渐广泛,流传形式逐渐多样,时至今日该故事已成为中国最具代表性的创世传说,具有丰富的文化意义。

Pangu was regarded as the creator of the universe in the mythology. "After he died, the parts of his body became the elements of the nature, his breath the wind and clouds, his voice the rolling thunder, his left eye the sun and the right eye the moon... his sweat flowed like rain and dew that **nurtured**④ all things on earth". The records reflect his great spirits of selfless **dedication**⑤ to human beings.

作为神话传说中的创世始祖,盘古"垂死化身,气成风云,声为雷霆,左眼为日,右眼为月……汗流为雨泽"的故事,体现出其为造福人类无私奉献的伟大精神。

In the multi-god country where people advocate nature, the Han people believe in Pangu as a personified deity. Many ethnic minorities in the south embrace him as a **totem**⑥. The people of Miao and Yao regard him as their ancestor. These reflect the feelings of the "ancestor worship" of the ancient Chinese. This kind of ancestor worship is not for an individual, but a deep experience and admiration for collective wisdom and **supreme**⑦ character of the ancestors. It is a worship of the spirit of the Chinese nation.

在崇尚自然的多神之国,汉族人民将盘古视为人格化的神灵,南方许多少数民族将其供奉为图腾,苗族、瑶族更是以盘古为祖先。这些都体现出中华古人的"祖先崇拜"情怀。这种祖先崇拜不是个人崇拜,而是对祖先集体智慧与至上品格的深度体验与推崇,是对中华民族精神的崇拜。

佳句点睛 Punchlines

1. Pangu Created Heaven and Earth is the most representative mythology of creation in China.

盘古开天地是中国最具代表性的创世神话传说。

2. The mythology of Pangu Created Heaven and Earth represents his great spirits of selfless dedication to the human beings.

盘古开天地的神话传说体现了盘古为造福人类无私奉献的伟大精神。

3. Pangu Created Heaven and Earth **reflects**⑧ the feelings of ancestor worship of the ancient Chinese.

盘古开天地体现出中国古人的祖先崇拜情怀。

情景对话 Situational Dialogue

A: Hello, boys and girls! Today we'll learn *Pangu Created Heaven and Earth*. Do you know this tale? Xiaoming, can you tell us something about it?

B: Yes, I can. This is a mythology of China and Pangu was the creator of the universe.

A: Good. Sit down, please. Li Man, can you add to it?

C: Yes, I can. Long long ago, the sky and the earth were not yet separated, and the universe was all chaos. The universe was like a big black egg, carrying Pangu inside itself. After eighteen thousand years, Pangu woke from a long sleep. He felt **suffocated**⑨, began to break the shell with an ax and stuck out his head and upper body.

A: Very good. Sit down, please. From their **presentation**⑩, we can see you have previewed the text very well. And now, let's learn this myth together.

A：同学们好！今天我们学习《盘古开天地》。你们知道这个故事吗？小明，你能跟我们说一说这个故事吗？

B：能。这是我国的一个神话传说，盘古是创造人类世界的始祖。

A：很好，请坐。李曼，你能补充一下吗？

C：好的。很久以前，天和地还没有分开，宇宙混沌一片。宇宙就像一个大黑蛋，把盘古包在里面。一万八千年后，盘古从长眠中醒来。他感到窒息，就用一把斧头劈开了蛋壳，探出了头和上身。

A：很好，请坐。从他们的回答中，可以看出同学们都对课文进行了很好的预习。现在，让我们一起来学习这个神话故事。

 生词注解　Notes

① mythology /mɪˈθɒlədʒɪ/　*n.* (统称)神话；虚幻的想法

② chronicle /ˈkrɒnɪkl/　*n.* 编年史；纪事

③ significance /sɪgˈnɪfɪkəns/　*n.* (尤指对将来有影响的)重要性；意义

④ nurture /ˈnɜːtʃə(r)/　*vt.* 养育；培养

⑤ dedication /ˌdedɪˈkeɪʃn/　*n.* 奉献；(书、音乐或作品前部的)献词

⑥ totem /ˈtəʊtəm/　*n.* 图腾；图腾形象

⑦ supreme /suːˈpriːm/　*adj.* (级别或地位)最高的；至高无上的

⑧ reflect /rɪˈflekt/　*vt.* 反映；映出(影像)

⑨ suffocate /ˈsʌfəkeɪt/　*vt.* 使……窒息而死；把……闷死

⑩ presentation /ˌpreznˈteɪʃn/　*n.* 介绍；陈述

女娲补天

Nvwa Patched up the Sky

  导入语　Lead-in

女娲是一位美丽的创世女神，人称"娲皇"或"女阴娘娘"。她开世造物，是华夏民族的人文始祖。女娲补天的相关传说在上古奇书《淮南子·览冥训》《列子·汤问》中均有记载。其中《淮南子·览冥训》写道："往古之时，四极废，九州裂……"在这种危机四伏的情况下，女娲决心熔炼彩石以补苍天，斩鳌足以立四极，从而留下了补天的动人传说。女娲不仅是补天的英雄，还是一尊创造万物的自然神。女娲补天的神话传说体现出了中国古代劳动人民探索自然、征服自然和改造自然的强烈愿望。

文化剪影　Cultural Outline

In ancient time, when the four pillars that **propped**① up the sky **collapsed**②, the earth **ruptured**③. Neither could the sky cover the whole earth, nor the earth contain all the creatures. Burning fire and **surging**④ water never ceased, so cruel beasts **endangered**⑤ human beings. Then Nvwa killed beasts for people's safety and begun to smelt the colored stones to mend the sky. Finally, the earth became as calm as before with the continuous efforts of Nvwa.

远古时期,四根擎天大柱倾倒,大地崩裂,天无法覆盖大地,大地也无法承载万物。大火不熄,洪水不止,凶猛的野兽危害着人类。于是,为了人类的安全,女娲杀死野兽,并冶炼五彩石来修补苍天。在她的不断努力下,大地最终恢复了往日的平静。

Nvwa Patched up the Sky is a well-known **mythology**⑥, quoted in the first chapter of *A Dream of Red Mansions*, one of the four great classical novels of ancient China. The myth of Nvwa patched the sky highlighted her important position as the great goddess of the universe. After her hard work and struggle, people began to live in harmony with nature.

女娲补天是一个家喻户晓的神话,中国古代四大名著之一《红楼梦》的第一回就引用了这个故事。女娲补天的神话彰显了她作为宇宙大神的重要地位,经过她的辛勤劳动和奋力拼搏,人与自然开始和谐相处。

Until now, during the first month of the lunar year, some Chinese people hold a seven-day large-scale temple fairs and sacrificial ceremonies in the memory of Nvwa, looking forward to good weather, peace and happiness in the coming year.

时至今日,在中国的一些地方,每年正月都要举行一场长达七天的大型庙会和祭祀活动,以此纪念女娲,并期盼来年风调雨顺、安乐和平。

佳句点睛 Punchlines

1. Nvwa Patched up the Sky shows the fearless fighting spirit of ancient Chinese.

女娲补天体现了中国古代人民大无畏的斗争精神。

2. The myths and legends of Nvwa Patched up the Sky have been handed down among the people for a long time, adding a colorful touch to the Chinese culture.

女娲补天的神话传说在民间流传甚久,为华夏文化添上了浓墨重彩的一笔。

3. The legend of Nvwa Patched up the Sky represents the rich imagination of the working people of ancient China.

女娲补天的传说体现了中国古代劳动人民丰富的想象力。

情景对话 Situational Dialogue

A: Emma, I find the Chinese myth stories are so interesting that I love them so much.

B: Sure. Which one do you like best?

A: Well, it's really a tough choice. Every myth is full of magic.

B: That's right. I love reading *Nvwa Patched up the Sky*.

A: Wow, Nvwa was so **miraculous**①. She did her best to patch the crumbling sky and protect human beings. In the Chinese ancients' mind, Nvwa was a Goddess who saved all the things in the world.

B: Yes, what a great Goddess she was!

A: 爱玛,我觉得中国神话故事很有意思,我太喜欢了。

B: 确实如此。你最喜欢哪一个神话?

A: 真是太难选择了,每一个神话故事都很神奇。

B: 说得没错,我喜欢读《女娲补天》。

A: 哎呀,女娲太不可思议了!她拼尽全力补天来保护人类,对中国古人来说是女娲挽救了世间万物。

B: 是啊,她是一位了不起的女神!

生词注解 Notes

① prop /prɒp/ *vt.* 支撑;使……倚靠在某物上

② collapse /kəˈlæps/　vi. 倒塌；崩溃

③ rupture /ˈrʌptʃə(r)/　v. 断裂；破裂

④ surge /sɜːdʒ/　vi. 汹涌；蜂拥而来

⑤ endanger /ɪnˈdeɪndʒə(r)/　vt. 危及；使……遭到危险

⑥ mythology /mɪˈθɒlədʒi/　n. (统称)神话；虚幻的想法

⑦ miraculous /mɪˈrækjələs/　adj. 神奇的；不可思议的

女娲造人

Nvwa Created Human Beings

导入语 Lead-in

女娲造人是中国上古神话传说之一,古籍中最早记载女娲造人故事的是《风俗通义》(又名《风俗通》)。《太平御览》《神话故事新编》等详述了女娲造人的具体过程。传说女娲初创世时,在造出了鸡狗猪牛马之后,于第七天造出了人,因此这一天被称为"人日"。相传女娲以泥土仿照自己的形象抟土造人,创造并构建人类社会。女娲还是人类得以延续的婚姻之神,她创立婚姻制度,使男女婚配,繁衍后代。女娲是中华民族的母亲,她慈祥地创造了生命,又勇敢地照顾生灵免受天灾,是被民间长久崇拜的创世神和始母神。女娲文化源远流长，是史前文明和中华民族优秀的传统文化，在古文化序列中占有非常重要的地位。

文化剪影　Cultural Outline

According to folklore, there were no human beings in the beginning of the world, so Nvwa made clay **figurines**① on her own image. Not only that, in order to let human beings continue to reproduce, she created the wedding ceremony, making people rely on their own power to carry on the lineage.

民间传说天地开辟之初，大地上并没有人类，女娲就仿照自己的形象，亲手用泥土捏造了人。不仅如此，为了让人类不断繁衍，她还创造了嫁娶之礼，让人们凭借自己的力量传宗接代。

Nvwa's love, hard work and **unremitting**② efforts showed the image of an **industrious**③, intelligent and great mother, who was full of vitality and **maternal**④ life, of a mother's joy and sorrow; and this kind of noble maternal love is the very source of our human circle of life.

女娲的慈爱、辛苦与不懈努力展现出一位勤劳、智慧、伟大的母亲形象，她充满生命的活力与母性，具有母亲的喜与忧，这种崇高的母爱正是我们人类生生不息的源泉所在。

Nvwa **graciously**⑤ created life, **courageously**⑥ kept living beings from natural disasters and was widely and long **worshipped**[7] as a Creator Deity.

女娲慈祥地创造了生命,又勇敢地照顾生灵免受天灾,被民间广泛而长久地尊为创世神。

佳句点睛　Punchlines

1. Nvwa was a great goddess in the primitive Chinese myths.
女娲是中国上古神话中的一位伟大女神。

2. Nvwa has been **honored**[8] as the "Mother of the earth".
女娲被尊称为"大地之母"。

3. The myth of Nvwa Created Human Beings has run a long history in China.
女娲造人的神话在中国源远流长。

情景对话　Situational Dialogue

A: Hi, David.

B: Hi, Mr. Wang. I wanna borrow a book on Nvwa.

A: Okay. Wait a moment. Do you know more about Nvwa?

B: Not too much. I heard she created human beings by herself.

A: Yeah. That's so magic. It is said that Nvwa was a goddess with a human head and a snake body in ancient Chinese myth.

B: Wow, I wonder how she created human beings.

A: Well, she used clay to pinch figurines firstly. But you can read more from this book.

B: Oh, I can't wait to read it.

A: 你好, 大卫。

B: 你好, 王先生。我想借一本有关女娲的书。

A: 好的, 稍等。你对女娲的故事了解多少?

B: 不太了解。我听说是她创造了人类。

A: 是呀, 很神奇! 在中国上古神话中, 女娲据说是一位人首蛇身的女神。

B: 哇, 我很好奇她是怎样创造人类的。

A: 起初她是用泥土捏出小小的泥人, 你可以从这本书中了解到更多的故事。

B: 哎呀, 我都迫不及待地想读这本书了。

生词注解　Notes

① figurine /ˌfɪɡəˈriːn/　n. 小雕像;小塑像

② unremitting /ˌʌnrɪˈmɪtɪŋ/　adj. 不懈的;不停的

③ industrious /ɪnˈdʌstriəs/　adj. 勤劳的;勤奋的

④ maternal /məˈtɜːnl/　adj. 母性的;母亲的;母系的

⑤ graciously /ˈgreɪʃəslɪ/ *adv.* 和蔼地;仁慈地

⑥ courageously /kəˈreɪdʒəslɪ/ *adv.* 勇敢地;英勇地

⑦ worship /ˈwɜːʃɪp/ *vt.* 崇拜;尊崇

⑧ honor /ˈɒnə(r)/ *vt.* 尊敬;给……以荣誉

大禹治水

Yu the Great Combated the Flood

 导入语 Lead-in

　　大约四千多年前,黄河流域发生了一场特大洪灾,水患给人民带来了无尽灾难。面对滔滔洪水,人们束手无策,只能逃到山上去躲避。许多人背井离乡,流离失所。起初,尧任命大禹的父亲鲧治理水患。鲧采取"水来土掩"的方法治水,但是未能成功。后来,大禹临危受命,担当此任,从鲧治水的失败中吸取教训,改堵为疏,体现出超凡的聪明才智。为了治理洪水,大禹置个人利益于不顾,"三过家门而不入"。大禹殚精竭虑,治水十三年,终于不负众望地完成了治水大业。

文化剪影 Cultural Outline

The story of Yu the Great Combated the Flood was a great event that happened at the end of the **primitive**① society of China. Together with the people, Yu the Great fought against natural disasters and **channeled**② floods with his labor and wisdom, showing his **extraordinary**③ leadership and infinite wisdom.

大禹治水的故事发生在中国原始社会末期,它是一件影响深远的大事。大禹与民众一起,用勤劳和智慧与自然灾害抗争,疏导洪水,体现出其非凡的领导才能和无穷的聪明才智。

It is recorded in *Mencius, Duke Wen of Teng I*, "Yu worked outside for eight years, passed his house three times and never went in." He was a truly hero who saved the nation and people. The story of Yu the Great Combating the Flood embodies Chinese **personification**④ of spirit of fearlessness and hard work.

《孟子·滕文公上》记载:"禹八年在外,三过家门而不入。"他是一位救国救民的真正英雄。大禹治水的故事体现了中国古代劳动人民不畏艰险、勤劳勇敢的民族精神。

It took thirteen years for Yu the Great to control the flood; it was he who made the people live a happy life. So the **posterity**⑤ built many temples for Yu the Great in memory of his contribution to them, and he has been honored as "God Yu". Even now, the myth, poetry and ballads about Yu the Great combating the flood are much-told in some parts of China.

大禹治水历时十三年,终于让人民过上了幸福生活。后代为了纪念他的功绩,为他广修庙宇,尊称他为"禹神"。至今,在中国的一些地方,人们还在传颂着许多有关大禹治水的传说、诗词和歌谣。

佳句点睛 Punchlines

1. Yu the Great was a best-known hero of combating the flood in the Chinese history.

大禹是中国历史上著名的治水英雄。

2. The amazing tales about Yu the Great Combated the Flood have been widely **eulogized**⑥ all the time for over thousands of years.

几千年来,大禹治水的神奇故事一直被广泛流传。

3. Yu the Great is the personification of resourcefulness, **perseverance**⑦ and selfless devotion.

大禹被视为足智多谋、不屈不挠和无私奉献的化身。

情景对话 Situational Dialogue

A: Good morning, Miss Li. I'm John. Could you tell me more about Yu the Great? I know he was a great hero of combating the flood in the ancient China.

B: Good morning, John. The legend of Yu the Great Combated the Flood is told from generation to generation in China. He was a fantastic hero in people's mind. Through thirteen years of **unremitting**® efforts, he and people finally completed dredging channels to lead the floodwaters to the sea.

A: Dear me! That's a long time.

B: So it is. It is said that he passed his house three times and never went in.

A: Gosh, what an incredible person! Thank you for telling me so much about the story of Yu the Great.

B: My pleasure.

A: 李老师,早上好!我是约翰。您能告诉我一些有关大禹的故事吗?我知道他是中国古代一位了不起的治水英雄。

B: 约翰,早上好!大禹治水的传说在中国代代相传,他是人们心目中的大英雄。他和人民一起疏通河道,经过十三年的不懈努力,成功把洪水引向了大海。

A: 我的天呀!时间真久!

B: 确实如此,据说他三过家门而不入呢。

A: 天哪,真是一个不可思议的人!谢谢您告诉我这么多有关大禹的故事。

B: 不客气。

生词注解 Notes

① primitive /ˈprɪmətɪv/ *adj.* 原始的;远古的

② channel /ˈtʃænl/ *vt.* 开辟水道;引导

③ extraordinary /ɪkˈstrɔːdnrɪ/ *adj.* 非凡的;特别的

④ personification /pəˌsɒnɪfɪˈkeɪʃn/ *n.* 人格化

⑤ posterity /pɒˈsterətɪ/ *n.* 后代;子孙

⑥ eulogize /ˈjuːlədʒaɪz/ *vt.* 颂扬;讴歌

⑦ perseverance /ˌpɜːsəˈvɪərəns/ *n.* 坚持不懈;不屈不挠

⑧ unremitting /ˌʌnrɪˈmɪtɪŋ/ *adj.* 不懈的;持续不断的

神农尝百草

Shennong Tasted Hundreds of Herbs

导入语　Lead-in

神农尝百草的故事是一则著名的中国古代传说。神农氏本是三皇之一,他看到鸟儿衔种而发明了五谷农业,因此被称为"神农氏"。在他所处的上古时代,还没有发明医药,先民们生病后只能等死。为了改变现状,神农氏上高山、钻老林,亲口尝遍了各种野草、树皮和种子,体察它们的药性,辨别它们的相互关系。根据积累的经验,他用草药为生病的先民治疗,取得了一定成效并口传了相关治疗方法,后经秦汉时期众多医学家搜集、整理而成《神农本草经》。《神农本草经》是中国现存最早的药经专著,也是对中国中草药的第一次系统总结,中医药学由此产生。

文化剪影 Cultural Outline

The story of Shennong Tasted Hundreds of Herbs is a beautiful story, which has been **eulogized**① for thousands of years. He tasted all kinds of herbs in person, healed the wounded and rescued the dying. In the struggle against nature and diseases, his accumulated experiences laid a foundation for the development of later generations' medical undertakings.

神农尝百草是一则美丽动人的传说,千百年来传颂至今。神农氏亲尝百草,救死扶伤。在与自然和疾病的斗争中,他积累的经验为后世医药事业的发展奠定了基础。

Shennong, a legendary figure in the traditional Chinese medicine history, overcame all the difficulties of nature with his wisdom. The discovery of herbs has a **fundamental**② effect on saving life and curing diseases.

作为中医药史上一位传奇般的人物,神农氏凭借着自己的智慧战胜了自然界中的种种困难。草药的发现对于救死扶伤、治疗疾病起到了至关重要的作用。

Later generations **compiled**③ *Shennong's Herbal Classic* based on the experiences passed down from Shennong. It is the earliest classic of Chinese herbal medicine in China. It has always had a positive **impaot**④ on the development of traditional Chinese medicine and gradually developed into a treasure in the world civilization.

后人根据神农氏总结出来的经验编著了《神农本草经》，它是中国现存最早的药经专著，对中医药学的发展一直产生着积极的影响，并逐步发展成为世界文明中的瑰宝。

佳句点睛 Punchlines

1. The story of Shennong Tasted Hundreds of Herbs reflects the **indomitable**⑤ and selfless **dedication**⑥ of the Chinese nation.

神农尝百草的故事体现了中华民族百折不挠、无私奉献的伟大精神。

2. As the founder of agriculture and medicine, Shennong left behind a valuable **legacy**⑦ for future generations.

作为农业和医药的创始者，神农氏为后人留下了宝贵的财富。

3. "Shennong tasted hundreds of herbs and got poisoned for seventy times each day", which is the perfect portrayal of his great virtue.

"神农尝百草，日遇七十毒"是对神农氏高尚品德的完美写照。

情景对话 Situational Dialogue

A: Guys, whoever knows the most wins. Are you ready?
B&C: Yes!

A: Here we go! Who created the world?

C: Pangu.

A: Great! Who tasted all kinds of herbs first?

B: Shennong.

C: Who was Shennong?

B: He was an amazing person. In Chinese ancient time, the people were **beset**® by various diseases and did nothing but to waited for dying. At that time, Shennong began to taste all sorts of herbs in jungles for saving people's lives. Gradually, traditional Chinese medicine emerged.

C: I love this story so much.

A: 朋友们,谁知道的最多,谁就是赢家。准备好了吗?

B&C: 准备好了!

A: 开始喽!是谁开辟了天地?

C: 盘古。

A: 好极了!谁第一个亲尝百草呢?

B: 神农氏。

C: 神农氏是谁?

B: 他可是一位了不起的人物呢!在中国古代,人们经常被各种疾病困扰,除了等死别无他法。神农氏为了挽救百姓的生命,深入山林去亲尝百草,中医药学也由此应运而生。

C: 我好喜欢这个故事!

生词注解 Notes

① eulogize /ˈjuːlədʒaɪz/ vt. 传颂；颂扬

② fundamental /ˌfʌndəˈmentl/ adj. 重要的；根本的

③ compile /kəmˈpaɪl/ vt. 汇编；编制

④ impact /ˈɪmpækt/ n. 巨大影响

⑤ indomitable /ɪnˈdɒmɪtəbl/ adj. 不屈不挠的；不服输的

⑥ dedication /ˌdedɪˈkeɪʃn/ n. 奉献；献身

⑦ legacy /ˈleɡəsɪ/ n. 遗产；遗赠

⑧ beset /bɪˈset/ vt. 困扰；包围

愚公移山

Foolish Old Man Removed the Mountains

 Lead-in

愚公移山是一个具有朴素唯物主义和朴素辩证法思想的寓言故事,出自《列子·汤问》。故事讲述的是愚公家门前有两座大山挡路,他决心把山铲平。另一位"聪明"的老人智叟笑他太傻,认为他根本办不到。但是,愚公带领儿孙不畏艰难、坚持不懈、挖山不止,最终感动了天帝,天帝命令夸娥氏的两个儿子搬走了两座大山。愚公的形象充分展现了中国古代劳动人民移山填海的坚定决心和顽强毅力。

文化剪影 Cultural Outline

Foolish Old Man Removed the Mountains is an old myth, which is **engraved**① the Chinese people's **conviction**② and widely retold till now. Though it is a myth, it reflects the people's **majestic**③ spirit of changing the nature at that time.

愚公移山是一个古老的神话故事，铭刻在世世代代华夏儿女的信仰之中，流传至今。虽然这是神话故事，但却反映了当时人们勇于改造自然的雄伟气魄。

The myth of Foolish Old Man Removing the Mountains brimmed with romanticism, it makes the grand ambition of Foolish Old Man come true by the divine power and mirrored the good wish of ancient Chinese people.

愚公移山的神话传说充满了浪漫主义色彩，愚公借助神力实现了宏伟抱负，表达了中国古代劳动人民的美好愿望。

"Foolish Old Man Removed the Mountains" is widely used as an idiom to describe the **unremitting**④ transformation of nature and **unswerving**⑤ struggle. Foolish Old Man's spirit of willpower and **perseverance**⑥ in dealing with difficulties has inspired generations of Chinese people to strive for continuous self-improvement.

如今，"愚公移山"作为一个被广泛使用的成语，用来描述坚持不懈地改造自然和坚定不移地进行斗争。愚公坚定不移、不畏艰难的精神毅力激励着一代又一代中国人民自强不息。

佳句点睛 Punchlines

1. The myth of Foolish Old Man Removed the Mountains realized his great ambition by virtue of the divine power.

愚公移山的神话传说借助神力实现了愚公的伟大抱负。

2. The myth of Foolish Old Man Removed the Mountains reflects the great spirit and amazing perseverance of the ancient Chinese laboring people in **transforming**⑦ nature.

愚公移山的神话传说反映了中国古代劳动人民改造自然的伟大气魄和惊人毅力。

3. Foolish Old Man is considered an honorable elder with perseverance and **foresight**⑧.

人们认为愚公是一位坚忍不拔、目光长远的可敬长者。

情景对话 Situational Dialogue

A: Hi, Mark. Today we learned a myth named *Foolish Old Man Removed the Mountains* in the Chinese class.

B: How did the tale begin?

A: Well, once upon a time, there was an old man named Foolish

Old Man. He lived in front of two high mountains. It was very difficult for his family to get in and out.

B: Then what happened?

A: The old man then led the whole family and started to remove the mountains by themselves. But a shrewd old man named Wise Old Man laughed that it was too foolish to move them away. Foolish Old Man told him, "As long as my **offspring**⑨ and I work hard every day, there will be a day when we can make it." Afterwards, the God was so moved by Foolish Old Man's action and **determination**⑩ that he commanded two of his followers to carry away the two mountains.

B: Wow, where there's a will, there's a way.

A: 你好，马克。今天语文课上，我们学习了《愚公移山》的神话故事。

B: 故事的开头是什么？

A: 嗯，很久以前，有一位名叫愚公的老人，他家门前有两座高山，阻碍了一家人的出入。

B: 然后呢？

A: 于是，愚公带领家人一起，想用自己的力量把大山移走。但是，另一位名叫智叟的聪明老人却取笑愚公的做法太愚蠢，无法搬走大山。愚公对他说道："只要我和子孙后代坚持不懈地努力，总有一天会成功的。"后来，天神被愚公的行动和决心所感动，吩咐两位手下把两座大山背走了。

B: 哇，真是有志者事竟成啊。

生词注解 Notes

① engrave /ɪnˈɡreɪv/ vt. 镌刻；铭记

② conviction /kənˈvɪkʃn/ n. 坚定的看法（或信念）

③ majestic /məˈdʒestɪk/ adj. 庄严的；宏伟的

④ unremitting /ˌʌnrɪˈmɪtɪŋ/ adj. 不懈的；坚忍的

⑤ unswerving /ʌnˈswɜːvɪŋ/ adj. 坚定不移的；始终不渝的

⑥ perseverance /ˌpɜːsəˈvɪərəns/ n. 坚持不懈；不屈不挠

⑦ transform /trænsˈfɔːm/ vt. 变换；改变

⑧ foresight /ˈfɔːsaɪt/ n. 远见；深谋远虑

⑨ offspring /ˈɒfsprɪŋ/ n. 后代；子孙

⑩ determination /dɪˌtɜːmɪˈneɪʃn/ n. 决心；坚定

嫦娥奔月

Chang'e Flew to the Moon

 导入语 Lead-in

嫦娥奔月是中国古代的神话传说,也是中国古代十大爱情故事之一。流传最广的版本是,嫦娥偷吃了西王母赐给她丈夫后羿的不死药后,飞到了月宫。月宫中虽

然是琼楼玉宇,但高处不胜寒。中国传统节日中秋节做月饼供嫦娥的风俗,便由此而来。至今,嫦娥奔月图仍经常出现在月饼包装袋上。嫦娥奔月的神话既表现出古人对星辰的崇拜,也反映出世人渴望美好团圆和幸福生活的情感。

 文化剪影　Cultural Outline

A bright moon **provided**① a beautiful space for the imagination of the ancient people. The tale that Chang'e Flew to the Moon has been passed down to this day and is well known by people. It's a good wish to know more about the moon.

明月为古人提供了一个唯美的想象空间。嫦娥奔月的故事流传至今,为人们所熟知。它表达了人们想了解月亮的美好愿望。

The legend of Chang'e flew to the moon has had a **profound**② impact on Chinese culture, and it contains a kind of mythological spirit yearning for freedom.

嫦娥奔月的传说对中国文化产生了深远的影响,它蕴含着一种向往自由的神话精神。

Now mankind have entered **cosmic**③ space and made a successful landing on the moon. However, the myth of Chang'e Flying to the Moon that ancient Chinese created still has its **unique**④ artistic **charm**⑤.

如今,人类已经进入宇宙空间,成功登月。但是,古代人民创作的嫦娥奔月的神话依然具有独特的艺术魅力。

佳句点睛 Punchlines

1. In Chinese mythologies, Chang'e, a great beauty, is not only a fairy in the moon, but also a holy goddess who can bring **auspiciousness**[6] for people.

在中国神话中,嫦娥美貌非凡,不仅是月宫仙子,还是能给人们带来吉祥的圣洁女神。

2. The mythology of Chang'e Fled to the Moon is favored by people from generation to generation, because of its charming beauty.

嫦娥奔月的故事之所以受到世世代代人们的青睐,是因为其中蕴含着动人的美。

3. A bright moon symbolizes a fond story, as well as means people's pursuit and yearning for all **marvelous**[7] things.

一轮明月既象征一个美好的故事,也意味着人们对一切美好事物的追求与向往。

情景对话 Situational Dialogue

A&B: Happy Mid-autumn Festival, Ms. Li.

C: Happy Mid-autumn Festival, girls.

A: Ms. Li, I heard that the festival came into being in memory of

Chang'e. Who was Chang'e?

C: Well, she was Houyi's wife in Chinese mythology.

B: I know a little about the traditional myth. But I have no idea why she flew to the moon alone.

C: There are various **versions** about the myth, and I'll tell you one popular version in China. Once upon a time, a man named Houyi and his beautiful wife named Chang'e lived happily. One day, Houyi got an **elixir** from the Queen Mother in heaven, yet Chang'e swallowed the elixir secretly, flew to the moon immediately and became a fairy.

B: Wow, what a special story.

C: Yeah. Then the Mid-autumn Festival came into being, representing the reunion just like the full moon.

A&B: 李老师，中秋节快乐！

C: 女孩子们，中秋节快乐！

A: 李老师，我听说中秋节是为了纪念嫦娥。嫦娥是谁？

C: 在中国神话故事里，她是后羿的妻子。

B: 我大致知道这个神话故事，但我不清楚嫦娥为什么独自飞去了月宫。

C: 这个故事有很多种版本，我给你们讲个流传较广的版本吧！很久以前，后羿和他的妻子嫦娥幸福地生活在一起。一天，后羿从天宫的王母娘娘那里得到一颗仙丹，但嫦娥偷吃了它，立即飞到月亮上成了仙。

B: 哇,好一个特别的故事。

C: 是呀,这就是中秋节的由来,中秋如同满月一般代表着团圆。

生词注解 Notes

① provide /prəˈvaɪd/   *vt.* 提供;准备

② profound /prəˈfaʊnd/   *adj.* 深远的;深切的

③ cosmic /ˈkɒzmɪk/   *adj.* 宇宙的;极广阔的

④ unique /juˈniːk/   *adj.* 独特的;独一无二的

⑤ charm /tʃɑːrm/   *n.* 魅力;魔力

⑥ auspiciousness /ɔːˈspɪʃəsnəs/   *n.* 吉祥;吉兆

⑦ marvelous /ˈmɑːvələs/   *adj.* 美妙的;非凡的

⑧ version /ˈvɜːʃn/   *n.* 版本;说法

⑨ elixir /ɪˈlɪksə(r)/   *n.* 灵丹妙药;长生不老药

后羿射日

Houyi Shot down the Suns

   导入语　Lead-in

后羿射日是中国远古神话传说。千百年来,后羿射日的壮举为人们所称道。最早的文字记录出现在战国时期楚国大夫屈原的《楚辞·天问》,比较完整的记录则出现在淮南王刘安及其门客编写的《淮南子》当中。在这部作品中,后羿被塑造成一位上射太阳、下杀猛兽,救万民于水火的英雄人物。后羿射日的故事集中体现了中国古代劳动人民想要战胜自然和改造自然的美好愿望。

文化剪影　Cultural Outline

The myth that Houyi Shot down the Suns has undergone a long period of development and changes, its content constantly enriched. It is one of the colorful myths in China. To a certain extent, it reflects the **unique**① personality and cultural characteristics of the Chinese nation.

后羿射日的神话故事经历了漫长的发展和变化，内容不断丰富，是中国多姿多彩的神话故事之一，在一定程度上折射出中华民族的独特个性和文化特征。

As a legendary **figure**② of Chinese mythology, Houyi was extraordinarily brave. He shot down nine suns and saved people from monstrous disasters, showing the great spirit that human beings can triumph over nature.

作为中国神话传说中的一位传奇人物，后羿神勇非凡。他射掉九个太阳，把人们从巨大的灾难中解救出来，体现出人类战胜自然的伟大精神。

The tale that Houyi Shot down the Suns was a unique, rare and surreal mythology. However, because of its **surrealism**③, the plot of this myth is more tortuous and legendary.

后羿射日是一个稀奇罕见的超现实神话。然而，正是因为其超现实的特点，所以这个神话的故事情节才显得更加曲折传奇。

 佳句点睛　Punchlines

1. Houyi Shot down the Suns is a kind of understanding and imagination of natural phenomena of ancient Chinese people.

后羿射日是中国古人对自然现象的一种理解与想象。

2. Houyi Shot down the Suns shows the courage of the ancient people fighting against nature, challenging nature, and conquering nature.

后羿射日反映了古人对抗自然、挑战自然和战胜自然的勇气。

3. The myth that Houyi Shot down the Suns reflects the **valiant**④ and **dauntless**⑤ quality of Houyi.

后羿射日的神话体现了后羿勇敢无畏的品质。

 情景对话　Situational Dialogue

A: It's a hot day, isn't it?

B: Yeah. I'm gonna suffer **sunstroke**⑥.

A: Is everything OK?

B: Thanks, I'm all right. There's only one sun in the sky after all. You know there were ten suns in the ancient times. That was so horrible.

A: A myth? Could you tell me more about it?

B: OK. So many people died of heatstroke and **dehydration**⑦ and all the plants couldn't survive, either. Everything was almost destroyed by heat.

A: Dear me! I can't imagine that terrible world.

B: At that time, a young man named Houyi wanted to save the world, so he shot down the nine **blazing**® suns with his arrows, keeping one sun in the sky to give its warmth and light. Finally, people could live again as before.

A: An incredible myth, an incredible hero.

A: 今天很热,是吧?

B: 是。我快要中暑了。

A: 你还好吗?

B: 谢谢,我还好。毕竟天上只有一个太阳嘛。你知道吗?古时候天上有十个太阳,那才可怕呢!

A: 这是神话传说吧?你能再讲一些吗?

B: 没问题。那时候许多人因中暑和脱水而死亡,所有植物也都无法幸免。炎热几乎毁灭了一切。

A: 天啊! 我简直无法想象那样恐怖的世界。

B: 此时,一个叫后羿的年轻人想拯救世界,于是他用箭射掉了九个炽热的太阳,只留一个太阳在天上发光发热。最后,人们又能像以前一样生活了。

A: 一个不可思议的神话,一位不可思议的英雄。

生词注解 Notes

① unique /juˈniːk/ *adj.* 独具的；特有的

② figure /ˈfɪɡə(r)/ *n.* 重要人物；身影

③ surrealism /səˈriːəlɪzəm/ *n.* 超现实主义

④ valiant /ˈvælɪənt/ *adj.* 英勇的；勇敢的

⑤ dauntless /ˈdɔːntləs/ *adj.* 无所畏惧的；吓不倒的

⑥ sunstroke /ˈsʌnstrəʊk/ *n.* 日射热；中暑

⑦ dehydration /ˌdiːhaɪˈdreɪʃn/ *n.* （身体）失水；脱水

⑧ blazing /ˈbleɪzɪŋ/ *adj.* 酷热的；炽热的

夸父追日

Kuafu Chased the Sun

导入语 Lead-in

夸父追日是中国著名的上古神话故事之一，出自《山海经·海外北经》。传说夸父是峨眉山上夸父族的一位首领，他身材魁梧、力大无穷，具有惊人的毅力。为了弄清太阳在一年四季对农作物的影

响，让人们合理利用阳光、熟悉自然规律，夸父拿一根桃木棍先从东到西测量日影、定四季，再标出黄河、渭河的最高涨水水位，为农作物提供耕种参考。可以说，夸父是中国农业科学的鼻祖。夸父追日是为了给人类采撷火种，使大地获得光明与温暖。夸父追日的故事极富想象力，同时也充满了浪漫主义的魅力。

文化剪影 Cultural Outline

The myth that Kuafu Chased the Sun uses the **exaggerated**① **techniques**② of expression and rich imagination, which make people **admire**③ the legend of the myth. In the long history and culture of China, Kuafu has always been a hero that people **look up to**④.

夸父追日的神话运用夸张的表现手法、丰富的想象,不得不让人赞叹神话故事的传奇。在中国历史文化的长河中,夸父始终是人们敬仰的英雄。

Though Kuafu Chased the Sun was not successful, it left the **posterity**⑤ with the majestic spirit of conquering nature and the spirit of desperate sacrifice, and has become one of the Chinese mythological stories full of miraculous colors.

虽然夸父追日没有成功,但它给后人留下了征服自然的雄伟气魄与奋不顾身的牺牲精神,成为充满神异色彩的中国神话故事之一。

Though Kuafu Chased the Sun was a brief myth, it has a strong symbolic meaning, displaying the ancient Chinese people's thinking about life and time.

夸父追日虽然是一个简短的神话故事,却具有强烈的象征意义,表现了中国古代人民对于生命和时间的思考。

佳句点睛 Punchlines

1. Kuafu Chased the Sun embodies his great spirit of **unyielding**[⑥] exploration of nature.

夸父追日体现了他不屈不挠探索自然的伟大精神。

2. Although Kuafu failed, but in the hearts of **descendants**[⑦], he is still an **esteemed**[⑧] and beloved hero.

夸父虽然失败了,但在后人的心中,他依然是受人们敬重与爱戴的英雄。

3. In a sense, Kuafu Chased the Sun reflects the spirit in which people strive for **eternal**[⑨] life.

从某种意义上说,夸父追日反映了人们为了追求永恒的生命奋斗不止的精神。

情景对话 Situational Dialogue

A: Mom, could you tell me a story? I can't sleep.

B: Of course, my baby. Let me see...er, what about Kuafu Chased the Sun?

A: OK, mom.

B: Long long ago, there were a group of people in the north of

China who lived in a mountain. Kuafu was the **chieftain**① of these people. One year, the weather was so hot that crops and trees died, and there was no water in rivers. People of Kuafu's tribe died one by one. Kuafu was so sad that and he determined to have a race with the sun and catch up with it. So he rushed in the direction of the sun. However, he was very tired and thirsty along the way, and finally he fell down forever.

A: Mom, I love Kuafu.

B: He's an amazing hero. OK, it's time for bed, good night, baby.

A: Good night, mom.

A: 妈妈，我睡不着。你能给我讲个故事吗？

B: 可以呀，宝贝。让我想想……呃，夸父追日怎么样？

A: 好啊，妈妈。

B: 很久很久以前，在中国北部的一座山上住着一群人，他们的首领叫夸父。有一年，天气炎热，庄稼和树木都干死了，河里没有一滴水。夸父部落里的人们接连死去。夸父很伤心，他决定去追赶太阳，于是就朝着太阳的方向出发了。但是途中他又累又渴，最后永远地倒下了。

A: 妈妈，我喜欢夸父。

B: 他是一位令人惊叹的英雄。好了，该睡觉了。晚安，宝贝。

A: 晚安，妈妈。

生词注解　Notes

① exaggerated /ɪɡˌzædʒəˈreɪtɪd/　*adj.* 夸张的；夸大的

② technique /tekˈniːk/　*n.* 技巧；手法

③ admire /ədˈmaɪə(r)/　*vt.* 钦佩；赞美

④ look up to　敬仰；尊敬

⑤ posterity /pɑːˈsterətɪ/　*n.* 子孙后代；后裔

⑥ unyielding /ʌnˈjiːldɪŋ/　*adj.* 不屈的；坚强的

⑦ descendant /dɪˈsendənt/　*n.* 后代；后裔

⑧ esteem /ɪˈstiːm/　*vt.* 尊重；敬重

⑨ eternal /ɪˈtɜːnl/　*adj.* 永恒的；不朽的

⑩ chieftain /ˈtʃiːftən/　*n.* 酋长；首领

精卫填海

Jingwei Filled up the Sea

导入语　Lead-in

精卫填海，出自《山海经·北山经》，是中国著名的上古神话传说之一。相传，炎帝神农氏的小女儿女娃溺亡于东海，死后其不平的灵魂化作一只花头、白嘴、红爪的神鸟，每天从山上衔来石头和草木，投入东海，发出"精卫、精卫"的悲鸣，立志填平东海。精卫填海的神话彰显了中国古代劳动人民征服自然的渴望和改变生存状态的勇敢精神。

文化剪影　Cultural Outline

Jingwei Filled up the Sea is one of the well-known and touching myths in China. People not only sighed about Emperor Yan's youngest daughter who was devoured by the **surging**① waves and then her spirit turned into a bird named Jingwei, but also touched by the **tenacious**② spirit of Jingwei carrying **twigs**③ and pebbles to fill up the sea.

精卫填海是中国古代神话中既家喻户晓又感人至深的故事之一。世人既因炎帝小女儿被海浪吞噬化成精卫鸟而叹息,更为精卫鸟衔运木石以填海的顽强精神而感动。

As a typical heroine with tragic color, Jingwei determined to fill up the sea by herself, day after day, year after year. What she did was probably in vain, but the **gritty**④ determination was more powerful than the sea.

精卫是一个典型的具有悲剧色彩的女主人公,她依靠个人意志,抱着填平沧海的决心,日复一日、年复一年地劳作着。虽然她的付出可能徒劳无益,但她坚韧不拔的决心比大海还要浩大。

Totem worship is a special **phenomenon**⑤ that has lasted for thousands of years in the Chinese history, so the myth of Jingwei Filling up the Sea not only reflects people's treasure on life, but also embodies a **totemic**⑥ culture. To a certain extent, it shows people's bird totemic beliefs in ancient times.

中国故事

图腾崇拜是中国历史上一种绵延数千年的特殊现象，精卫填海的神话故事不仅表现了人类对生命的珍惜，也是图腾文化的一种体现。在一定程度上，它展示了远古时期人们的鸟图腾信仰。

佳句点睛 Punchlines

1. The myth of Jingwei Filled up the Sea **demonstrates**⑦ that a spirit to resist and sacrifice bravely.

精卫填海的神话故事体现了一种敢于反抗、勇于牺牲的精神。

2. Although the sea is **mighty**⑧, the gritty spirit of Jingwei is greater.

沧海固然大，但精卫坚韧不拔的决心更伟大。

3. The myth of Jingwei Filled up the Sea has a tragic beauty, which has been shocking the people's hearts for thousands of years.

精卫填海的神话故事有一种悲壮之美，千百年来一直震撼着人们的心灵。

情景对话 Situational Dialogue

A: Hi, Lisa. You don't look happy, what's up?

B: Hi, Lily. My Chinese teacher gave so many **assignments**⑨. That's why I'm unhappy.

A: Cheer up, Lisa! Jingwei could fill up the sea by herself in ancient times, so nothing is difficult in the world.

B: Jingwei? I have no idea about the person.

A: She was a character of Chinese myths. One day she was drowned in the sea. After death, she turned into a bird. Every day, she kept carrying twigs and pebbles to fill up the sea tirelessly. Jingwei had great determination to do that, so what about you?

B: Thank you very much, Lily. I think I know how to do next.

A: My pleasure. Good luck to you!

A: 你好,丽莎。你看起来不太开心,怎么了?

B: 你好,莉莉。我的汉语老师布置了好多作业,所以我一点都不开心。

A: 振作一点,丽莎!古时候的精卫都能把海填平,所以这个世界上没有什么难事。

B: 精卫?我不知道这个人是谁。

A: 她是中国神话故事中的一个人物。有一天,她淹死在了大海里。她死后化为一只鸟,每天不知疲倦地衔来细枝和石块以填平大海。精卫面对这样困难的任务尚有如此大的决心,而你只遇上这么一点小困难。

B: 多谢,莉莉。我知道接下来该怎么做了。

A: 不客气。祝你好运!

生词注解 Notes

① surge /sɜːdʒ/ v. 汹涌；涌动

② tenacious /təˈneɪʃəs/ adj. 顽强的；坚韧的

③ twig /twɪɡ/ n. 细枝；嫩枝

④ gritty /ˈɡrɪtɪ/ adj. 坚定的；坚毅的

⑤ phenomenon /fəˈnɒmɪnən/ n. 现象；杰出的人才

⑥ totemic /təʊˈtemɪk/ adj. 图腾的

⑦ demonstrate /ˈdemənstreɪt/ vt. 证明；证实

⑧ mighty /ˈmaɪtɪ/ adj. 巨大的；非凡的

⑨ assignment /əˈsaɪnmənt/ n. (分派的)工作；任务

民间故事 第一部分

钻木取火

Drill the Wood to Get Fire

导入语 Lead-in

钻木取火的故事来源于中国古代的神话传说。相传远古时期,河南商丘一带是一片森林。在森林中居住的燧人氏经常捕食野兽,当击打野兽的石块与山石相碰时常常产生火花,他因而受到启发,就折下燧木枝摩擦生热,生出火来。他把这种方法传授给其他人,人类从此学会了人工取火,并开始用火烤制食物、照明、取暖、冶炼等,人类生活从此开始了一个崭新的纪元。后来,人们称这位圣人为"燧人氏",尊他为"三皇之首"。钻木取火的神话传说反映了原始社会人们的生活从生食到熟食的进化过程,也展示了古人无尽的想象和智慧。

 文化剪影　Cultural Outline

Drilling the wood to get fire is based on the principle of heat **generated**① by **friction**②. The wood itself is **rough**③, and in the process of constant friction will produce heat the wood itself is **flammable**④, so there will be a fire.

钻木取火是基于摩擦生热的原理。因为木材本身较为粗糙,在不断摩擦的过程中会产生热量,而木材本身就是易燃物,所以就会生出火来。

How to use fire is a **significant**⑤ **milestone**⑥ in the human history. The invention of drilling the wood to get fire not only represents the wisdom and strength of ancient Chinese people, but makes a start on Chinese civilization.

火的使用是人类历史上一个重要的里程碑,钻木取火的发明不仅代表了中国古代劳动人民的智慧和力量,也开启了华夏文明。

Fire culture has existed in China for thousands of years, and the ancient civilization of making fire by drilling the wood is now no longer in existence. Fortunately, this ancient technology is still alive and well in the Li **ethnic**⑦ region of China, where it has become a **distinct**⑧ feature.

火文化在中国经历了数千年的历史,而钻木取火这项古老的文明如今已不复存在。幸运的是,在中国黎族地区至今还保留着这项古老的技术，它已经成为当地的鲜明特色。

佳句点睛 Punchlines

1. The invention of drilling the wood to get fire ended a period that human beings ate the **raw**⑨ meat of birds and beasts, starting a new era of human civilization.

钻木取火的发明结束了人类茹毛饮血的时代，开创了人类文明的新纪元。

2. Fire not only brings light to humanity, but also civilization.

火不仅给人类带来了光明，也带来了文明。

3. Drilling the wood to get fire is a revolutionary result of human conquest of nature.

钻木取火是人类征服自然的革命性成果。

情景对话 Situational Dialogue

A: Good morning, what can I do for you?

B: Good morning, I wanna buy a book about Chinese mythologies.

A: OK, this way, please. What about this one?

B: Let me see. Well, I'll take it. Frankly speaking, I'm interested in the skill of drilling the wood to get fire.

A: That's really an amazing Chinese invention. The wood gradually produced sparks as it continued rubbing.

A&B: Then a new world came to earth.

B: Perfect! But the old invention has disappeared now.

A: Not really. People in the Li ethnic region of Hainan Province still retain this technology.

B: Wow, that's so **incredible**⑩.

A:早上好,有什么能为您服务的吗?

B:早上好,我想买一本关于中国神话的书。

A:好的,请这边走。这本怎么样?

B:让我看看。好,就要这本了! 坦率地说,我对钻木取火这项技能十分感兴趣。

A:那真是一个了不起的中国发明。木头在不断摩擦的过程中就渐渐产生了火花。

A&B:然后人类生活从此开始了新纪元。

B:完美! 不过,这项古老的发明已不复存在了。

A:不见得。海南省黎族地区的人们至今还保留着这项技术。

B:天啊,太不可思议了。

生词注解　Notes

① generate /ˈdʒenəreɪt/　*vt.* 使……形成;发生

② friction /ˈfrɪkʃən/ n. 摩擦；摩擦力

③ rough /rʌf/ adj. 粗糙的；不平滑的

④ flammable /ˈflæməbl/ adj. 易燃的；可燃的

⑤ significant /sɪɡˈnɪfɪkənt/ adj. 有重大意义的；显著的

⑥ milestone /ˈmaɪlstəʊn/ n. 里程碑；转折点

⑦ ethnic /ˈeθnɪk/ adj. 民族的；种族的

⑧ distinctive /dɪˈstɪŋktɪv/ adj. 独特的；有特色的

⑨ raw /rɔː/ adj. 生的；未烹制的

⑩ incredible /ɪnˈkredəbl/ adj. 不可思议的；难以置信的

仓颉造字

Cangjie Created Chinese Characters

  导入语 Lead-in

仓颉，原姓侯冈，名颉，人称"仓颉先师"，又称"史皇氏""苍王""仓圣"，黄帝时期的史官。仓颉造字是中国古代神话传说之一。仓颉造字于陕西洛南，造字的地方叫"凤凰衔书台"。仓颉是中国的"造字圣人"，他根据野兽的脚印和自然现象研究出了文字，并对流传于先民中的文字加以搜集、整理和使用，可以说他是汉字的规范者、整理者和统一者，在汉字创造的过程中起到了至关重要的作用。

文化剪影 Cultural Outline

Cangjie was a legendary figure. According to the legend, he looked up at the sky and tracked birds, animals, insects, and fish, creating China's most primitive **hieroglyph**①, which ended the uncivilized age of keeping records by tying knots, then it gradually developed into the modern Chinese characters. So Cangjie is **honored**② as "The Ancestor of Creating Chinese Characters".

仓颉是一位具有传奇色彩的人物。传说他仰观天象,俯察鸟兽虫鱼的踪迹,创造出中国最原始的象形文字,从而结束了远古时期结绳记事的蒙昧时代,象形文字逐渐演变成了今天的汉字。因此,仓颉被尊称为"造字始祖"。

Cangjie creating Chinese characters ended the history of people keeping records by tying knots, and created a **precedent**③ for Chinese civilization, making human beings enter a new era with Chinese characters. So Chinese characters are the carrier of the Chinese nation's five thousand-year civilization, history and culture.

仓颉造字结束了人们结绳记事的历史,开创了中华文明的先河,使人类进入有文字记载的文明时代。因而,汉字是中华民族五千年文明与历史文化的载体。

The ancients regarded Cangjie Created Chinese Characters as a **shocking**④ event, created many strange **phenomena**⑤ and **trans-**

formed⑥ Cangjie into a half-man and half-god image, which reflects ancient people's worship for Chinese characters.

古人把仓颉造字的事迹当作一件惊天地泣鬼神的大事,虚构出了许多奇异的现象,还把仓颉神化为半人半神的形象,这也正说明了古人对文字的崇拜。

佳句点睛　Punchlines

1. The mythology of Cangjie Created Chinese Characters reflects the infinite wisdom and **striking**⑦ creativity of ancient people.

仓颉造字的神话体现了古人无穷的智慧和惊人的创造力。

2. Cangjie **normalized**⑧ and arranged Chinese characters by himself.

仓颉亲自规范和整理了文字。

3. Chinese characters is one of the old characters in the world, which is called "The God of Longevity".

汉字是世界上古老的文字之一,堪称"老寿星"。

情景对话　Situational Dialogue

A: Good afternoon, everyone.
B: Good afternoon, Mr. Zhao.

A: We'll continue to learn *Cangjie Creating Chinese Characters* this afternoon. Who can tell us this myth? Liu Jinjin, please.

B: Cangjie was a legendary figure, who is honored as the sage of creating Chinese characters.

A: Good. Please sit down. Wang Kai, please.

C: In ancient times, people kept records by tying knots. Big knots represent big things, and small ones stand for trifles. But the more things happen, the messier the knot gets. Then Cangjie found the footprints of animals, and he was **inspired**① by traces of all kinds of animals to create the earliest form of Chinese characters.

A: Well done. Sit down, please.

A: 同学们,下午好!

B: 赵老师,下午好!

A: 今天下午我们接着学习《仓颉造字》。谁能给我们讲一下这个神话?请刘金金同学来回答。

B: 仓颉是一个传奇人物,他被后世尊称为"造字圣人"。

A: 好,请坐下。王凯同学请说!

C: 古时候,人们结绳记事,大结代表大事,小结代表小事。可是,事情越多,结也变得越混乱。后来,仓颉发现了一些动物的脚印,受到动物脚印的启发创造了汉字的雏形。

A: 非常好,请坐下。

中国故事

生词注解 Notes

① hieroglyph /ˈhaɪərəɡlɪf/ n. 象形文字；象形符号

② honor /ˈɒnə(r)/ vt. 尊敬；给……以荣誉

③ precedent /ˈpresɪdənt/ n. 先例；前例

④ shocking /ˈʃɒkɪŋ/ adj. 令人震惊的；触目惊心的

⑤ phenomena /fəˈnɒmɪnə/ n. (phenomenon 的复数) 现象

⑥ transform /trænsˈfɔːm/ vt. 转化；变换

⑦ striking /ˈstraɪkɪŋ/ adj. 引人注目的；显著的

⑧ normalize /ˈnɔːməlaɪz/ v. 使……标准化；常规化

⑨ inspire /ɪnˈspaɪə(r)/ vt. 使……产生灵感；启发

牛郎织女

Cowherd and Weaving Girl

 导入语　Lead-in

　　牛郎织女是中国古代著名的民间爱情故事,也是中国四大民间爱情传说之一。牛郎织女的故事最早起源于星辰崇拜,由牵牛星、织女星的星名演化而来,与该传说相关的节日是七夕节。牛郎织女的故事雏形最早见于《诗经》:"维天有汉,监亦有光。跂彼织女,终日七襄。虽则七襄,不成报章。睆彼牵牛,不以服箱。"其中出现了有关织女、牵牛星宿的记载,一直以来被认为是牛郎织女传说的萌芽。南朝梁殷芸《小说》中记载:"天河之东有织女,天帝之女也,年年机杼劳役,织成云锦天衣,容貌不暇整。天帝怜其独处,许嫁河西牵牛郎,嫁后遂废织纴。天帝怒,责令归河东,许一年一度相会。涉秋七日,鹊首无故皆髡,相传是日河鼓与织女会于河东,役乌鹊为梁以渡,故毛皆脱去。"后经人们的加工,最终形成了优美动人的神话故事。

文化剪影 Cultural Outline

The legend of Cowherd and Weaving Girl tells us a beautiful and heart-breaking love story. It is believed that Cowherd and Weaving Girl have been silently guarding each other on either side of the Milky Way, witnessing the valuable spirit that "life is precious, love is more valuable". With the passage of time, this myth can be called as a touching story with Chinese cultural characteristics with its increasingly rich plots and **diversified**[①] forms of expression.

牛郎织女的传说讲述了一段凄美动人的爱情故事。人们相信,牛郎织女一直在天河两侧默默地守护着对方,见证着"生命诚可贵,爱情价更高"的可贵精神。随着时间的推移,这段神话传说的情节不断丰富,表现形式也更加多样化,堪称具有中华民族文化特色的动人故事。

The myth of Cowherd and Weaving Girl is full of romantic feelings and peculiar imagination, which reflects people's desire for love and the beautiful yearning for family life. It is a traditional story with the classic culture of the Chinese nation, which contains profound national culture. Meanwhile, the folk culture phenomenon derived from the story continues to this day.

牛郎织女的神话充满了浪漫的情怀和奇特的想象,反映了人们对爱情的渴望以及对家庭生活的美好向往。它是一个传达中华民族经典文化的传统故事,蕴含着深厚的民族文化,由该故事衍生出的民俗文化现象延续至今。

The day on July 7 of the **lunar**② calendar each year is named "Qi Xi". It is said that Cowherd and Weaving Girl can be reunited on the bridge that the **magpies**③ formed annually, and this day is also called Chinese Valentine's Day by modern people. In some **rural**④ areas of China, people would stand under a grapevine that night, because they believe that they can **overhear**⑤ the couple are whispering. The love story of Cowherd and Weaving Girl is so wonderful and touching, so people still often use the term "Cowherd and Weaving Girl" to describe the love between husband and wife.

每年的农历七月初七,俗称"七夕",相传是牛郎织女一年一度在鹊桥上相会的日子,这一天还被现代人誉为中国的情人节。在我国的一些农村地区,人们会在七夕当夜站在葡萄架下面,据说可以偷听到牛郎织女的悄悄话。因为牛郎织女的爱情故事美妙动人,所以直到今天,人们还常常以"牛郎织女"来描述恩爱的夫妻。

佳句点睛 Punchlines

1. The loyal love between of Cowherd and Weaving Girl has moved the **descendants**⑥ through thousands of years.
牛郎织女之间忠贞不渝的爱情在千年之后依然动人。

2. The myth of Cowherd and Weaving Girl encourages young people's determination and courage to **pursue**⑦ the beautiful love.

牛郎织女的神话激励着青年男女勇于追求美好爱情。

3. The myth of Cowherd and Weaving Girl is the earliest love story on stars in China.

牛郎织女的神话是中国最早关于星辰的爱情故事。

情景对话　Situational Dialogue

A: Hi, Mr. Zheng. Could I ask you a question?

B: Hi, Mary. Please!

A: We has Valentine's Day in western countries, so do you have any festivals about lovers?

B: Of course. We have Chinese Valentine's Day on July 7 of the lunar calendar each year.

A: Wow! Tell me more, please.

B: The Chinese Valentine's Day is about a couple named Cowherd and Weaving Girl. The male was a cowherd who lived in a village and the female was a girl weaver who lived in heaven. One day they fell in love with each other, then they married and gave birth to a boy and a girl. Unfortunately, the God of Heaven soon found out the fact and brought Weaving Girl back to heaven. Finally, the couple were separated on both sides of the Milky Way forever. The God of Heaven eventually[5] was moved, allowing them to meet every year on July 7 of the lunar calendar.

A: So that day is called Chinese Valentine's Day.

B: You're right.

A: 郑老师,您好! 我能问您一个问题吗?

B: 你好! 玛丽。请讲!

A: 在西方国家我们有情人节。你们有关于爱人的节日吗?

B: 当然有了。每年的农历七月初七是中国的情人节。

A: 哇! 请再给我介绍一些吧。

B: 中国的情人节是关于牛郎和织女这一对夫妇的。牛郎是生活在农村的牧牛人,织女是生活在天上的纺织仙女。一天,他们相爱了,后来结婚生育了一儿一女。不幸的是,天神很快发现了,要把织女带回天上去,这对夫妇被天上的银河永远地分开了。后来天神终于被他们的爱情所感动,允许他们在每年的农历七月初七那天相会。

A: 所以那天就被称为中国的情人节。

B: 说得对!

生词注解　Notes

① diversified /daɪˈvɜːsɪfaɪd/　*adj.* 多样化的;多样化的

② lunar /ˈluːnə(r)/　*adj.* 月亮的;月球的

③ magpie /ˈmæɡpaɪ/　*n.* 喜鹊

④ rural /ˈrʊərəl/　*adj.* 乡村的;农村的

⑤ overhear /ˌəʊvəˈhɪə(r)/ *vt.* 无意中听到；偷听到

⑥ descendant /dɪˈsendənt/ *n.* 后代；后裔

⑦ pursue /pəˈsjuː/ *vt.* 追求；追赶

⑧ eventually /ɪˈventʃuəlɪ/ *adv.* 最后；终于

白蛇传

The Legend of White Snake

 导入语 Lead-in

　　白蛇传的神话传说源远流长，最早记叙于明代文学家冯梦龙所著的《警世通言》。白蛇传是中国四大民间爱情传说之一，是中国民间集体创作的典范。它讲述了修行千年的白蛇化身为白娘子，携青蛇小青来到杭州西湖，与药店伙计许仙相遇、相恋、结姻，复遭和尚法海横加干涉等一系列悲欢离合的故事，表达了古代人民对男女自由恋爱的赞美和对封建势力束缚的有力鞭答。白蛇传的故事是浙江省杭州市地方传统民间文学，也是国家级非物质文化遗产之一。

文化剪影 Cultural Outline

The Legend of White Snake is a well-known tale among Chinese people, absorbing rich folk culture and **attaining**① its unique cultural status. This beautiful and **legendary**② story has experienced various forms of spreading, with a strong folk literature feature.

白蛇传是中国民间家喻户晓的传说，它汲取了丰富的民间涵养，具有独特的文化地位。这个优美而富有传奇色彩的故事经历了多种形式的传播，具有强烈的民间文学特色。

The Legend of White Snake is beautiful and moving, full of legend and romance. In particular, the kind-hearted and **unyielding**③ character of the heroine Bai Suzhen embodied in the traditional Chinese women has been eulogized. At the same time, the legend to a certain extent also reflects the emotional characteristics of the Chinese nation and artistic creativity.

白蛇传优美动人，充满了传奇性和浪漫色彩。尤其是女主人公白素贞身上体现的中国传统女性的善良、坚贞不屈的品格至今仍被人们颂扬。同时，该传说在一定程度上也体现了中华民族的情感特征和艺术创造力。

The folk customs of the Legend of White Snake are extremely rich, which has **essential**④ reference value for people to know about local customs and practices of southern regions of the Yangtze River.

For Hangzhou, the scene of the legend, its natural and cultural landscape—Leifeng **Pagoda**⑤ and the West Lake are closely related to the Legend of White Snake.

白蛇传中的民风民俗内容极其丰富,对人们了解江南的风土人情具有重要的参考价值。对于该传说的主要发生地杭州而言,白蛇传与雷峰塔、西湖等自然和文化景观形成了密不可分的关系。

佳句点睛　Punchlines

1. The Legend of White Snake is a shining pearl of Chinese folk literature.

白蛇传是中国民间文学中的一颗璀璨明珠。

2. The Legend of White Snake shows people's strong yearning for the liberation of humanity.

白蛇传表达了人们对人性解放的强烈渴望。

3. The Legend of White Snake is regarded as a treasure of the spiritual and cultural **heritage**⑥ of the Chinese nation.

白蛇传被称为中华民族宝贵的精神文化遗产。

情景对话　Situational Dialogue

A: Welcome to the West Lake. It's a famous freshwater lake in

Hangzhou, the capital of Zhejiang Province in eastern China. Now, you can see Leifeng Pagoda, which is one of the famous Scene Spots of the West Lake.

B: Any stories about the beautiful place?

A: Yes. It is said there was a white snake who was called Bai Suzhen. She was willing to repay Xu Xian for saving her life 500 years ago, then she **transformed**⑦ into a beautiful young lady and came to the world. Luckily, they met at the West Lake in Hangzhou by accident, so the young people fell in love with each other and got married. Shortly after that, a monk named Fa Hai found Bai Suzhen was a snake spirit, and he wanted to tear them apart. Then she was **confined**⑧ to Leifeng Pagoda by Fa Hai.

A: 欢迎大家来到西湖。它坐落于中国东部浙江省杭州市,是一个著名的淡水湖。现在你们看到的雷峰塔就是西湖著名景点之一。

B: 这么美丽的地方有什么故事吗?

A: 那是自然!据说有条白蛇叫白素贞,她为了报答五百年前挽救自己性命的许仙,化作一位美人来到人间。幸运的是,他俩在西湖偶然相遇了,这对年轻人很快就坠入爱河并结为夫妇。可是好景不长,一个叫法海的和尚发现了白素贞是个蛇精,他要把这对夫妇分开,于是就把白素贞压在了雷峰塔下。

生词注解　Notes

① attain /əˈteɪn/　vt. 获得；实现

② legendary /ˈledʒəndrɪ/　adj. 传奇的；传说的

③ unyielding /ʌnˈjiːldɪŋ/　adj. 坚定的；顽强不屈的

④ essential /ɪˈsenʃl/　adj. 极其重要的；必不可少的

⑤ pagoda /pəˈɡəʊdə/　n. (东方寺院的)宝塔

⑥ heritage /ˈherɪtɪdʒ/　n. 遗产(指国家或社会长期形成的历史、传统和特色)

⑦ transform /trænsˈfɔːm/　vt. 使……改变形态(或性质)；使……改观

⑧ confine /kənˈfaɪn/　vt. 禁闭；使……离不开

梁山伯与祝英台

Liang Shanbo and Zhu Yingtai

 导入语 Lead-in

梁山伯与祝英台是中国民间四大爱情传说之一，也是在世界上广泛流传的中国民间传说之一。自东晋开始，梁山伯与祝英台的故事在民间流传已有一千七百多年，可谓历史悠久、家喻户晓，被誉为爱情的千古绝唱。它歌颂了一对有情人敢于打破封建礼教的禁锢和束缚，坚守爱情，忠贞不渝，最终化蝶双飞的浪漫传奇故事。从古至今，无数人被梁山伯与祝英台的悲惨爱情所感染，反映了中国人对美好爱情的无限向往与追求。

文化剪影 Cultural Outline

The legend of Liang Shanbo and Zhu Yingtai is a treasure of Chinese culture. For thousands of years, it has been loved by people for its **circuitous**[①] and moving plots, **distinctive**[②] characters and wonderful story structure. Though the ending is sad, the story gives people a hazy hope.

梁山伯与祝英台的传说是中华文化的瑰宝。千百年来,它以曲折动人的情节、鲜明的人物特征和奇妙的故事结构而受到人们的喜爱。故事的结局虽然悲切,但又给人一种朦胧的希望。

As one of the four major folk legends of China, the romance of Liang Shanbo and Zhu Yingtai is known as "Romeo and Juliet" of the East. With the development of the times, the legend in the story and art form is improving day by day, with distinctive national characteristics.

梁山伯与祝英台是中国四大民间传说之一,被称为东方的"罗密欧与朱丽叶"。随着时代的发展,该传说在故事情节及艺术形式方面日臻完善,具有鲜明的民族特色。

The story of Liang Shanbo and Zhu Yingtai has been constantly enriched in the spread. In some places, many tombstones and temples with the legend as the theme have been built. In addition, a variety of literary and artistic works adapted from the legend **constitute**[③] the Liang Shanbo and Zhu Yingtai culture with Chinese characteristics.

梁山伯与祝英台的故事在流传中不断被丰富,有些地方甚至兴建了众多以梁祝传说为主题的墓碑和庙宇等建筑。此外,由该传说改编的多种文学艺术作品构成了具有中国特色的梁祝文化。

佳句点睛　Punchlines

1. The artistic **charisma**④ revealed in the myth of Liang Shanbo and Zhu Yingtai has enabled it to become a rarity of Chinese folk literature.

梁祝传说中所展现的艺术魅力,使其成为中国民间文学中的一件珍宝。

2. The legend of Liang Shanbo and Zhu Yingtai shows their undying beautiful love.

梁山伯与祝英台的传说体现了他们至死不渝的美好爱情。

3. Since ancient times, so many people have been **touched**⑤ by the sad but beautiful love between Liang Shanbo and Zhu Yingtai.

从古至今,有无数人被梁山伯与祝英台的凄美爱情所打动。

情景对话　Situational Dialogue

A: Wait a minute, Jack. Listen.

B: That's a piece of wonderful music—*Liang Shanbo and Zhu*

Yingtai, which is my favorite.

A: It sounds like Chinese names.

B: Right. The violin **concerto**⑥ is based upon a Chinese myth named Liang Shanbo and Zhu Yingtai, which is also called "Butterfly Lovers".

A: Is it a love story, then?

B: Yes. It happened in the **feudal**⑦ society, the two young people fell in love, but their love had a **zigzag**⑧ road, and finally both of them died for love. However, what surprising is that the two lovers **incarnated**⑨ butterflies, dancing together.

A: It's too sad, but I like their love story so much.

B: Me, too. OK, let's move on.

A: 等一下,杰克。听!

B: 是一首美妙的乐曲——《梁山伯与祝英台》,这是我的最爱。

A: 听起来像是中国人的名字。

B: 对。这首小提琴协奏曲是以中国的神话传说梁山伯与祝英台为基础的,梁祝也被称为"蝴蝶恋人"。

A: 这是一个爱情故事?

B: 是的。这个故事发生在封建社会时期,这两个年轻人相爱了。可是他们的爱情之路蜿蜒曲折,最后双双殉情。不过,令人惊讶的是,这对恋人化身为蝴蝶一起翩翩起舞。

A: 太悲伤了。不过,我很喜欢他们的爱情故事。

B: 我也是。好了,我们继续走吧。

生词注解　Notes

① circuitous /səˈkjuːɪtəs/　*adj.* 曲折的；迂回的

② distinctive /dɪˈstɪŋktɪv/　*adj.* 独特的；有特色的

③ constitute /ˈkɒnstɪtjuːt/　*vt.* 构成；组成

④ charisma /kəˈrɪzmə/　*n.* 魅力；感召力

⑤ touch /ˈtʌtʃ/　*vt.* 感动；触摸

⑥ concerto /kənˈtʃeətəʊ/　*n.* 协奏曲

⑦ feudal /ˈfjuːdl/　*adj.* 封建（制度）的

⑧ zigzag /ˈzɪɡzæɡ/　*adj.* 蜿蜒的；曲折的

⑨ incarnate /ɪnˈkɑːnət/　*vt.* 使……成化身；使……具体化

花木兰代父从军

Hua Mulan Joined the Army for Her Father

 导入语 Lead-in

　　花木兰是中国南北朝时期一位具有传奇色彩的巾帼英雄,她的故事是一首悲壮的英雄史诗。木兰从小练习骑射,恰逢皇帝招兵,木兰父亲的名字也在名册之中。然而父亲因年老多病而不能胜任,于是她便女扮男装,替父出征。花木兰的故事最早出现于南北朝叙事诗《木兰辞》中,"唧唧复唧唧,木兰当户织。不闻机杼声,惟闻女叹息……"花木兰代父从军的传奇故事传唱至今。

 文化剪影 Cultural Outline

The story that Mulan Joined the Army for Her Father first appeared in the famous ancient Chinese **folksong**① *Song of Mulan*. After the continuous development and changes, it has become rich in content gradually. Mulan's kindness, bravery and passion② for defending her country are still being sung about.

花木兰代父从军的故事最早出现于中国古代著名的民歌《木兰辞》中,经过不断地发展和演变,其内容越来越丰富。花木兰善良勇敢的品质和保家卫国的热情至今仍被人们所传唱。

Hua Mulan was a famous heroine in Chinese ancient legends. Her story was a heroic song and a tragic poem. The spirit of Mulan has **inspired**③ hundreds of millions of Chinese people to make great **feats**④ in the battles to defend their country.

花木兰是中国古代传说中一位家喻户晓的女英雄,她的故事是一首英雄的赞歌,一段悲壮的史诗。她的精神激励着亿万中华儿女在保家卫国的战斗中做出惊天动地的壮举。

Nowadays⑤, "Mulan" has become a kind of culture and spirit, and has entered the hearts of hundreds of millions of people. Mulan's legend has also been put on the screen, **extolled**⑥ by later generations, and even her spirit has gone to the world.

如今,"木兰"已经成为一种文化、一种精神,深入到亿万人的心中。木兰的传说也被搬上了荧幕,备受后人赞颂,她的精神甚至已经传播到世界各地。

佳句点睛 Punchlines

1. The legend that Hua Mulan Joined the Army for Her Father reflects the heroism of defending her country.
花木兰代父从军的传说体现了她保家卫国的英雄气概。

2. The heroic deed that Hua Mulan Joined the Army for Her Father are enduring.
花木兰代父从军的英雄事迹经久不衰。

3. The story that Hua Mulan Joined the Army for Her Father is tragic and heroic **epic**⑦.
花木兰代父从军的故事是一首悲壮的英雄史诗。

情景对话 Situational Dialogue

A: Alice, are you free tonight?

B: Yeah, I am. What plan do you have?

A: Why don't we go to see a movie named *Hua Mulan*?

B: *Hua Mulan*? What kind of the movie?

A: Well, the movie is based on the Chinese legend of Hua Mulan.

She was a legendary heroine who joined the army for her father and embodied the virtues of Chinese women.

B: I see. In 1998, the Disney Company adapted the story of Mulan into a **cartoon**③.

A: Yes. It's a classical movie. See you tonight at the cinema at nine o'clock.

B: OK. See you tonight.

A: 爱丽丝,你今晚有空吗?

B: 有空啊。你有什么安排吗?

A: 我们一起去看电影《花木兰》吧?

B:《花木兰》? 是什么类型的电影?

A: 嗯,这部电影是以中国传说花木兰为基础的。花木兰是一位代父从军的传奇英雄,她集中体现了中国女性的美德。

B: 我明白了。1998年,迪士尼公司曾将花木兰的故事改编成动画电影。

A: 是的,这是一部经典电影。今晚九点电影院见。

B: 好的,晚上见。

生词注解　Notes

① folksong /ˈfəʊk sɒŋ/　*n.* 民歌;民谣

② passion /ˈpæʃn/　*n.* 激情;热情

③ inspire /ɪnˈspaɪə(r)/　*vt.* 激励;鼓舞

④ feat /fiːt/ *n.* 功绩；英勇事迹
⑤ nowadays /ˈnaʊədeɪz/ *adv.* 现今；时下
⑥ extol /ɪkˈstəʊl/ *vt.* 颂扬；称赞
⑦ epic /ˈepɪk/ *n.* 史诗；叙事诗
⑧ cartoon /kɑːˈtuːn/ *n.* 动画片

第二部分　成语故事

Part II　Idiom Stories

三顾茅庐

Make Three Calls at the Thatched Cottage

导入语 Lead-in

三顾茅庐,典出《三国志·蜀志·诸葛亮传》:"先帝不以臣卑鄙,猥自枉屈,三顾臣于草庐之中。"东汉末年,天下纷争,汉朝宗亲刘备招贤纳士,听说诸葛亮很有才华,于是三次到诸葛亮的茅庐拜请。诸葛亮终于被刘备诚恳的态度打动,辅佐他成就光复汉室的大业。后来,在诸葛亮的帮助下,刘备很快壮大了势力。从此,三顾茅庐被传为佳话。

 文化剪影 **Cultural Outline**

Making Three Calls at the Thatched Cottage is not only a story from one of the four great classical Chinese novels—*The Romance of Three Kingdoms*, but also is a very common idiom in China. Nowadays, people often use it as a **metaphor**[①] of sincerely and repeatedly visiting **sages**[②] with **expertise**[③].

三顾茅庐不仅是中国四大名著之一《三国演义》中的一个典故，同样也是一个十分常用的中国成语。如今，人们常用其来比喻真心诚意，一再邀请、拜访有专长的贤人。

The story of Making Three Calls at the Thatched Cottage not only praises Liu Bei's spirit of seeking talents with eagerness and honoring worthy men of letters, but also reflects Zhuge Liang's brilliant talent with profound knowledge. The idiom is rich in cultural **connotation**[④], which embodies wishes and ideals of ancient intellectuals and has been **integrated**[⑤] into Chinese culture.

三顾茅庐的故事不仅赞扬了刘备求贤若渴、礼贤下士的精神，也体现了诸葛亮满腹经纶的才华。该典故具有丰富的文化内涵，体现了古代知识分子的愿望和理想，已经深深融入中国文化之中。

The story of Making Three Calls at the Thatched Cottage is very popular, and has become a familiar and frequently used literature **allusion**[⑥] and is regarded as a model of respecting talents. Even the folk built some temples about Liu Bei and Zhuge Liang to **commemorate**[7] them.

三顾茅庐的故事流传很广,已经成为一个人们耳熟能详、经常使用的典故,被视为尊重人才的典范。民间甚至还修建一些有关刘备、诸葛亮的庙宇,以示纪念。

佳句点睛　Punchlines

1. Throughout the history, the story of Making Three Calls at the Thatched Cottage is praised as an **eternal**[8] model of honoring worthy men of letters.

纵观历史,三顾茅庐被人们颂为礼贤下士的永久典范。

2. Zhuge Liang has been the embodiment of the wisdom of Chinese intellectuals for thousands of years.

几千年来,诸葛亮是中国知识分子智慧的化身。

3. The story of Making Three Calls at the Thatched Cottage is a wonderful part of *The Romance of Three Kingdoms*.

三顾茅庐是《三国演义》中的精彩华章。

情景对话 Situational Dialogue

A: Jack, I find Li Chenhao is a clever boy.

B: Yes. He's a "little Zhuge".

A: "Zhuge"? I don't quite understand.

B: To be **precise**①, it should be Zhuge Liang, who was an outstanding militarist, statesman and the symbol of wisdom in Chinese history. There's a classical story between Zhuge Liang and Liu Bei.

A: You know that I'm a story fan. Please go on.

B: OK. The name of the story is Making Three Calls at the Thatched Cottage, telling us that Liu Bei visited Zhuge Liang's cottage three times and wanted to invite him to be his military adviser. Finally, Zhuge Liang was moved by Liu Bei's sincerity and helped him **establish**② the kingdom of Shu.

A: Zhuge Liang was really a man full of wisdom. That is to say, if a person is very clever, he/she will be called "Zhuge Liang".

B: That's right.

A: 杰克,我发现李晨浩是个很聪明的孩子。

B: 是的,他就是个"小诸葛"。

A: "诸葛"? 我不太明白。

B: 确切地说,应该是诸葛亮。他是中国历史上出色的军事家、政治家,也是智慧的象征。他和刘备之间还有一个经典的故事呢!

A: 你知道，我是故事迷。请接着说。

B: 好。故事的名字叫三顾茅庐，说的是刘备三次去拜请诸葛亮，想请他当自己的军师；后来诸葛亮被刘备的诚意所打动，帮助刘备建立了蜀国。

A: 诸葛亮真是个充满智慧的人！也就是说，如果一个人很聪明，就可以被称为"诸葛亮"。

B: 说得对。

 ## 生词注解　Notes

① metaphor /ˈmetəfə(r)/　n. 隐喻；暗喻

② sage /seɪdʒ/　n. 贤人；智者

③ expertise /ˌekspɜːˈtiːz/　n. 专门知识或技能；专长

④ connotation /ˌkɒnəˈteɪʃn/　n. 含义；内涵

⑤ integrate /ˈɪntɪɡreɪt/　vt. 使……融入；使……一体化

⑥ allusion /əˈluːʒn/　n. 典故；暗示

⑦ commemorate /kəˈmeməreɪt/　vt. 纪念

⑧ eternal /ɪˈtɜːnl/　adj. 永久的；永恒的

⑨ precise /prɪˈsaɪs/　adj. 精确的；精密的

⑩ establish /ɪˈstæblɪʃ/　vt. 建立；创立

望洋兴叹

Lament One's Littleness before the Vast Ocean

 导入语　Lead-in

望洋兴叹,出自战国时期著名思想家庄周所著的《庄子·秋水》:"秋水时至,百川灌河。泾流之大,两涘渚崖之间,不辨牛马。于是焉,河伯欣然自喜,以天下之美为尽在己。顺流而东行,至于北海,东面而视,不见水端。于是焉河伯始旋其面目,望洋向若而叹曰……"意思是说,河伯因河水大涨而自以为了不起,后来到了海边,看到无边无际的大海,于是望洋而叹。这个成语原指在伟大事物面前感叹自己渺小,现在多比喻做事时因不能胜任或没有条件而感到无可奈何。这个故事对于人们正确认识客观世界具有一定的启迪意义。

文化剪影　Cultural Outline

The idiom of **Lamenting**① One's Littleness before the Vast Ocean is full of romantic color, which shapes the image of an enlightened person. By contrast it reveals the truth that there is always someone stronger and knowledge is infinite.

望洋兴叹这个成语故事极富浪漫主义色彩,塑造出一个觉悟者的形象;通过对比揭示出天外有天、学无止境的道理。

The idiom story of Lamenting One's Littleness before the Vast Ocean has profound **implications**②, which represents the **essence**③ of Zhuang Tzu's thought and tells people that the world is infinite and their understanding of the world is also endless.

望洋兴叹这个成语故事具有深刻的寓意,体现了庄子思想中的精华;同时也告诉人们世界是无限的,人对世界的认识也永无止境。

A short idiom story not only reveals profound truth, but also reflects the thoughts of the Chinese Taoist school that everything has its own certain laws, and these laws would change all the time.

一则简短的成语故事不仅揭示出深刻的道理,也反映了中国道家学派的思想,即万事万物都有一定规律,而这些规律又是时刻发生变化的。

 佳句点睛 Punchlines

1. The idiom of Lamenting One's Littleness before the Vast Ocean tells us not to be **arrogant**[④].

望洋兴叹这个成语告诉我们做人不要狂妄自大。

2. The idiom of Lamenting One's Littleness before the Vast Ocean made us realize that each of us is just a **speck**[⑤] of dust in front of the universe.

望洋兴叹这个成语让我们明白：在宇宙面前，我们每个人都不过是一粒微尘。

3. Only **modesty**[⑥] is the passport on the road to learning.

唯有谦虚才是学习道路上的通行证。

 情景对话 Situational Dialogue

A: Good evening, Tian Tian. It's Shelly is speaking.

B: Good evening, Shelly. What's up?

A: I asked for leave today, and I missed Chinese class. Can you tell me something about your study?

B: Sure. I studied an idiom story named Lamenting One's Littleness before the Vast Ocean.

A: Thank you, Tian Tian. Can you tell me the story briefly?

B: OK. Many years ago, there was a river **deity**① named Hebo who lived in the Yellow River, and he considered himself the greatest in the world. However, when he came to the North Sea along the river, looking to the east, he couldn't see the bounds of the sea. Then he looked at himself and felt he was so tiny and **insignificant**②. So Hebo sighed and realized his shortcomings.

A: Thank for telling me the story.

B: Not at all.

A: 晚上好,田甜。我是雪莉。

B: 晚上好,雪莉。有什么事吗?

A: 我今天请假了,没去上中文课。你能跟我说说学习了什么内容吗?

B: 当然可以。我们今天学习了一个成语故事——望洋兴叹。

A: 谢谢你,田甜。你能简短地给我讲一讲吗?

B: 好呀。很久以前,黄河的河神河伯自以为是天下至尊。但是,当他沿河来到北海时,朝东望去却看不到海的尽头;再反观自身才觉得自己是如此渺小,微不足道。于是,河伯叹了口气,意识到了自己的不足。

A: 谢谢你告诉我这个故事。

B: 不客气。

生词注解　Notes

① lament /ləˈment/　v. 悲叹；痛惜

② implication /ˌɪmplɪˈkeɪʃn/　n. 含意；暗指

③ essence /ˈesns/　n. 本质；精华

④ arrogant /ˈærəgənt/　adj. 傲慢的；自大的

⑤ speck /spek/　n. 小点；污点

⑥ modesty /ˈmɒdəstɪ/　n. 谦虚；谦逊

⑦ deity /ˈdeɪətɪ/　n. 神；女神

⑧ insignificant /ˌɪnsɪgˈnɪfɪkənt/　adj. 不重要的；无足轻重的

高山流水

High Mountains and Flowing Water

 导入语　Lead-in

《高山流水》是中国十大古曲之一，出自《列子·汤问》："伯牙鼓琴，志在高山。钟子期曰：'善哉，峨峨兮若泰山。'志在流水，曰：'善哉，洋洋兮若江河。'"俞伯牙每弹完一曲，钟子期总能心领神会，"辄穷其趣"。俞伯牙离琴叹道："善哉，善哉，阁下能听出曲中志趣，君所思即是我所思，我哪能隐藏得了我的心声呢？"两人遂成人生知己。钟子期去世后，伯牙痛失知音，摔琴绝弦，终身不弹。直至今日，"知音"依然用来形容朋友之间的默契与情谊，而"高山流水"则比喻知音难遇或乐曲高妙。

 文化剪影　Cultural Outline

"High Mountains and Flowing Water" is not only an ancient musical instrument, but also a popular well-known idiom. In this idiom, the bosom friend's **affection**① between Yu Boya and Zhong Ziqi brings people warmth and hope, so that many people yearn for it.

"高山流水"既是古琴名曲，又是大家熟知、广为流传的成语。这一成语故事中俞伯牙和钟子期的知音之情不仅给人以温暖，也给人以希望，令许多人心向往之。

The reason why the story of High Mountains and Flowing Water can be widely **circulated**② in the long river of history is that it's rich in cultural heritage. The cultural spirit of **harmony**③ between man and nature in ancient China is fully reflected in the much-told story.

高山流水的故事之所以在历史的长河中广为流传，是因为其包含了深厚的文化底蕴。中国古代天人合一的文化精神在这段佳话中得到了充分的体现。

The friendship between Yu Boya and Zhong Ziqi has **touched**④ countless generations. According to the legend, in the place where they met, an ancient Chinese **zither**⑤ platform was built. The idiom of High Mountains and Flowing Water can remind people of ancient legends and make people feel the shocking power of national culture.

俞伯牙和钟子期的友谊感动了无数后人。传说在他们相遇的地方,筑起了一座古琴台。高山流水这个成语既能让人想起那古老的传说,又能让人感受到民族文化的震撼力量。

佳句点睛 Punchlines

1. The story of High Mountains and Flowing Water is the most touching musical one in Chinese history.
高山流水是中国历史上最动人心弦的音乐故事。

2. The idiom of High Mountains and Flowing Water embodies the cultural spirit of "forgetting everything" in ancient China.
高山流水的成语故事体现了中国古代"物我两忘"的文化精神。

3. In China, mountains and waters have been symbols of traditional culture since ancient times.
在中国,山和水自古以来就是传统文化的一种象征。

情景对话 Situational Dialogue

A: Miaomiao, I heard a piece of music—*High Mountains and Flowing Water*, which sounds so wonderful.

B: Well, that's a famous song in China and also an idiom.

A: Really?

B: Yes. There's a story about it. Are you interested in it?

A: Yeah. I'm all ears.

B: It's said that Yu Boya was a famed music master, having superb skills in playing the musical instrument. When Boya played a piece of music **eulogizing**⑥ the high mountains, a man named Zhong Ziqi heard and said the melody was as **magnificent**⑦ and **dignified**⑧ as Mount Tai towering into the clouds. When Boya played a piece of music depicting the **turbulent**⑨ waves, Zhong Ziqi could also understand it. Since then they had been very good friends.

A: What profound Chinese culture!

B: Exactly.

A: 苗苗,我听了一首名叫《高山流水》的乐曲,简直太美妙了!

B: 嗯,那是一首中国名曲,而且还是一个成语呢。

A: 真的吗?

B: 是的。还有一个关于它的故事呢,有兴趣听吗?

A: 当然,洗耳恭听。

B: 据说俞伯牙是一位著名的琴师,琴艺高超。当伯牙弹起赞美高山的曲调时,被一个叫钟子期的人听到了,他说曲调雄伟庄重,好像高耸入云的泰山一般。当伯牙弹奏表现汹涌澎湃的波涛时,钟子期又能理解其曲意。从此,两人就成了非常要好的朋友。

A: 中国文化还真是博大精深啊!

B: 确实如此。

生词注解 Notes

① affection /əˈfekʃn/　n. 喜爱；钟爱

② circulate /ˈsɜːkjəleɪt/　vt. 传播；流传

③ harmony /ˈhɑːmənɪ/　n. 和谐；协调

④ touch /tʌtʃ/　vt. 感动；触动

⑤ zither /ˈzɪðə(r)/　n. 古筝；齐特琴

⑥ eulogize /ˈjuːlədʒaɪz/　vt. 称赞；颂扬

⑦ magnificent /mæɡˈnɪfɪsnt/　adj. 壮丽的；宏伟的

⑧ dignified /ˈdɪɡnɪfaɪd/　adj. 高贵的；有尊严的

⑨ turbulent /ˈtɜːbjələnt/　adj. 汹涌的；湍动的

破镜重圆

A Broken Mirror Joined Together

 Lead-in

破镜重圆,出自宋代李致远《碧牡丹》:"破镜重圆,分钗合钿,重寻绣户珠箔。"这个故事源于南朝陈亡时,驸马徐德言与其妻乐昌公主破一镜,各执一半为信物,并约定他日求合。后来,将军杨素掳去乐昌公主,使他们夫妇失散。此后,几经周折,杨素问明原委,便派人找来徐德言,成全了这对夫妻,使他们破镜重圆。这段佳话四处传扬,于是就有了破镜重圆的典故,用来比喻夫妻失散或分手后重新团圆、和好如初、言归于好。

文化剪影 Cultural Outline

The **allusion**① of A Broken Mirror Joined Together comes from a much-told story that Xu Deyan separated and **reunited**② with his wife. Although the couple went through **hardships**③, the spirit that they kept promise and the loyal love have been **eulogized**④ by literary men of all ages.

破镜重圆的典故源自徐德言与妻子分离而又重聚的佳话。这对夫妻虽历经患难,但他们信守约定、对爱情忠贞不渝的精神被历代文人歌颂。

The idiom story of A Broken Mirror Joined Together not only is a beautiful love story, but reflects the virtue of gentlemen help others to **fulfil**⑤ their wish. Now it represents people's good wish for love.

破镜重圆的成语故事不仅讲述了一个优美的爱情故事,更反映出君子成人之美的美德。现在它代表着人们对爱情的一种美好愿望。

Mirror is widely used as a literary image in traditional Chinese literature, which means perfection, brightness and cleanliness. The idiom of A Broken Mirror Joined Together refers to flawless love.

镜子是中国传统文学中一个被广泛使用的文学意象,它意味着圆满、明亮和洁净。成语破镜重圆是借镜子来比喻完美无瑕的爱情。

 佳句点睛 Punchlines

1. The **exceedingly**⑥ **sentimental**⑦ love story in the idiom of A Broken Mirror Joined Together has been eulogized by the gifted scholars and beautiful ladies of all times.

破镜重圆这个成语故事中缠绵悱恻的爱情一直为历代的才子佳人所讴歌。

2. The idiom of A Broken Mirror Joined Together is used to refer to the reunion of a couple after they lose touch or break up.

破镜重圆这个成语比喻夫妻失散或分离后重新相聚。

3. You left me with your half of the mirror, and now the mirror is back but not you.

镜与人俱去,镜归人未归。

 情景对话 Situational Dialogue

A: Who can tell me what's the meaning of a mirror in China?

B: One can see himself in a mirror, so maybe it means cleanliness.

A: Good. Sit down, please. What about you?

C: I think it means brightness.

A: In fact, there's an old story about it in China. In the Northern and Southern dynasties when the State of Chen was faced with its **demise**②, Xu Deyan, the emperor's son-in-law, broke a bronze mirror into halves, each of they kept a half as **tokens**② in case they were separated. Soon afterwards, the couple did lose sight of each other, but they were reunited by the half of the mirror each had kept. Then we'll learn an idiom about the story.

B&C: A Broken Mirror Joined Together.

A: Right.

A: 你们知道在中国镜子象征着什么吗?

B: 一个人可以透过镜子看到自己,所以它也许是洁净的意思吧。

A: 好,请坐。你认为呢?

C: 我想它意味着明亮。

A: 事实上,在中国有一个关于它的古老故事。南北朝时期的陈国将要灭亡时,驸马徐德言把一面铜镜破开,他与妻子各留下一半作为日后相见的凭证。后来,这对夫妇真的失散了,但凭借着各自留下的半面铜镜又得以团圆。今天我们要学习一个关于镜子的成语。

B&C: 破镜重圆。

A: 对。

生词注解 Notes

① allusion /əˈluːʒn/ *n.* 典故；影射

② reunite /ˌriːjuˈnaɪt/ *vt.* 使……重逢；使……再次相聚

③ hardship /ˈhɑːdʃɪp/ *n.* 艰难；困苦

④ eulogize /ˈjuːlədʒaɪz/ *vt.* 颂扬；称赞

⑤ fulfil /fʊlˈfɪl/ *vt.* 履行(诺言等)；达到(目的)

⑥ exceedingly /ɪkˈsiːdɪŋlɪ/ *adv.* 极其；非常

⑦ sentimental /ˌsentɪˈmentl/ *adj.* 充满柔情的；多愁善感的

⑧ demise /dɪˈmaɪz/ *n.* 终止；失败

⑨ token /ˈtəʊkən/ *n.* 象征；信物

名落孙山

Fall behind Sun Shan

 导入语　Lead-in

　　名落孙山，出自宋朝范公偁的《过庭录》："吴人孙山，滑稽才子也。赴举他郡，乡人托以子偕往。乡人子失意，山缀榜末，先归。乡人问其子得失，山曰：'解名尽处是孙山，贤郎更在孙山外。'"说的是从前有一位名叫孙山、能言善辩的才子。有一年，他去参加科举考试，公布名单时他是最后一名被录取的人。回到家里后，邻居向他打听自己儿子的考试情况。孙山笑着告诉邻居说，他考取了最后一名，而邻居儿子的名字还在他后面。从此，人们便根据这个故事把报考学校或参加考试没被录取叫作"名落孙山"。

文化剪影 Cultural Outline

After continuous development and changes, the story of Falling behind Sun Shan (failing in an competitive examination) has **evolved**① into a familiar idiom, which is widely used in daily life.

经过不断地发展与变化，名落孙山由故事逐渐演变成了现在大家熟知的成语，在日常生活中被广泛使用。

Sun Shan used humorous language to answer a difficult question, which embodies his **extraordinary**② wit and also vividly **reflects**③ the wisdom of life contained in traditional Chinese culture.

孙山用幽默的语言回答了一个令人难以回答的问题，体现了他过人的机智，也生动地反映了中国传统文化中所蕴含的人生智慧。

Sun Shan in the story of Falling behind Sun Shan answered the question in a **tactful**④ and funny way, which was not embarrassing, could **effectively**⑤ **convey**⑥ information.

名落孙山里的孙山以委婉风趣的方式回答问题，既不令人尴尬，又能有效传递信息。

佳句点睛 Punchlines

1. Sun Shan was a talented man with witty remarks.

孙山是一位说话诙谐风趣的才子。

2. People used the idiom of Fall behind Sun Shan to **indicate**⑦ failing in an examination or a competition.

人们用名落孙山来比喻考试没有考上或选拔未被录取。

3. The way of Sun Shan answering questions has a certain artistic expression of language.

孙山回答问题的方式具有一定的语言表达艺术。

情景对话 Situational Dialogue

A: OK. Thank you for listening. Who's next?

B: It's my turn.

A: Please!

B: Good morning, everybody. I'll tell you a story about examination today. In the Song Dynasty, there was a humorous man called Sun Shan. One year he went to take the examination, and his name showed the last on the list of successful **candidates**⑧. When Sun Shan came home, one of his neighbors asked him whether his son had also passed. Sun Shan said with a smile: "Sun Shan is the last on the list, and your son falls behind Sun Shan."

A: Thank you for telling us such an interesting story.

B: It's my pleasure.

A: 很好。谢谢大家的聆听！下一位是谁呢？

B: 到我了。

A: 有请！

B: 大家上午好！今天我要给大家讲一个有关考试的故事。宋朝时，有一位很幽默的人，名叫孙山。有一年，他参加了考试，公布名单时他是最后一名被录取的。回到家后，他的邻居向他打听自己儿子的考试情况，孙山笑着对邻居说："榜单上最后一名是孙山，你儿子的名字还在孙山后面呢。"

A: 感谢你为我们带来如此有趣的故事。

B: 不客气。

生词注解　Notes

① evolve /ɪˈvɒlv/　v. 使……逐渐形成；逐渐演变

② extraordinary /ɪkˈstrɔːdnrɪ/　adj. 不平常的；非凡的

③ reflect /rɪˈflekt/　vt. 反映；反射

④ tactful /ˈtæktfl/　adj. 圆通的；得体的

⑤ effectively /ɪˈfektɪvlɪ/　adv. 有效地

⑥ convey /kənˈveɪ/　*vt.* 表达；传递（思想、感情等）

⑦ indicate /ˈɪndɪkeɪt/　*vt.* 表明；显示

⑧ candidate /ˈkændɪdeɪt/　*n.* 应试者；候选人

才高八斗

A Person of Great Talent

才高八斗，出自《南史·谢灵运传》。说的是南朝文学家谢灵运，他出身东晋大士族，常常怀才不遇，但他写的山水诗却颇受人们青睐。一次酒热耳酣之际，谢灵运狂放不羁地说："天下才共一石，曹子建独得八斗，我得一斗，自古及今共分一斗。"意思是说，天下的文学之才共有一石（一石等于十斗），曹子建（曹植）独占了八斗，谢灵运占了一斗，天下其他人共占一斗。这就是人们常说的"才高八斗"的由来，由此可见曹植的才华与名气之高。从此以后，后世便称才学出众的人为"才高八斗"或"八斗之才"。

文化剪影　Cultural Outline

With the changes of the times, the story of A Person of Great Talent has gradually become a widely-used idiom. Its meaning has also changed, which **originally**① meant the **outstanding**② talent of Cao Zhi, then is used to describe a person rich in literary talent.

随着时代的变迁,才高八斗的故事逐渐成为一个广泛使用的成语,它的意思也随之发生了变化,由最初特指曹植才华出众,到现在多用于形容一个人富有文才。

The idiom story of A Person of Great Talent not only praises Cao Zhi's **extraordinary**③ literary talent, but also reflects the **self-conceited**④ character of Chinese **intellectuals**⑤ like Xie Lingyun to some extent.

才高八斗的成语故事不仅赞扬了曹植非凡的文学才华,也在一定程度上体现了像谢灵运一样的中国传统知识分子自命不凡的性格特征。

As a unit of **capacity**⑥ in ancient China, Dan was used to describe a person's talent and had a **distinctive**⑦ taste when read.

作为中国古代的一种容量单位,石被用来形容一个人的才华,读来别有一番趣味。

 佳句点睛 Punchlines

1. The idiom of A Person of Great Talent praises the **prodigious**[8] talent of Cao Zhi.

才高八斗这个成语赞扬了曹植的才华横溢。

2. The idiom of A Person of Great Talent is used to describe one person who is rich in literature and knowledge.

才高八斗形容一个人富有文才、知识丰富。

3. From the idiom story of A Person of Great Talent, we can see Cao Zhi's **distinguished**[9] talent and high reputation.

从才高八斗这个成语故事中，我们可以看到曹植的卓越才华和鼎鼎大名。

 情景对话 Situational Dialogue

A: Excuse me, may I ask you a question?

B: Go ahead, please.

A: Why do people use the Chinese idiom A Person of Great Talent to describe a talented person?

B: This idiom is based on a story about Cao Zhi, who was the third son of Cao Cao, a leader who lived during the Three Kingdoms period in ancient China. Cao Zhi, who was very intelligent and loved to study, wrote many outstanding articles, which showed his artistic talent and earned him the **admiration**② of a lot of people. Xie Lingyun said, "If there's one dan (equal to ten dou) of talent in the world, Cao Zhi alone has eight dou of it."

A: Cao Zhi was awesome.

B: Yes, if you have time to read his *Ode to Goddess Luo River*, you will see that it the case.

A: Well, I'll definitely read it.

A: 打扰一下,能请教您一个问题吗?

B: 请讲。

A: 为什么人们用成语才高八斗来形容一个人的才华?

B: 这个成语的来源与曹植有关。曹植是三国时期诸侯曹操的三儿子,他文采斐然,热爱学习,曾写过不少佳作,令世人赞叹不已。谢灵运曾说过:"如若天下文才共有十斗,曹植一人独占八斗。"

A: 曹植太牛了。

B: 是啊,有时间看看他写的《洛神赋》,你就明白此言不虚。

A: 好,我一定好好拜读一下。

生词注解　Notes

① originally /əˈrɪdʒənəlɪ/　*adv*. 原来;起初

② outstanding /aʊtˈstændɪŋ/　*adj*. 优秀的;杰出的

③ self-conceited /ˈselfkənˈsiːtɪd/ *adj.* 自负的；骄傲自大的

④ intellectual /ˌɪntəˈlektʃuəl/ *n.* 知识分子；脑力劳动者

⑤ extent /ɪkˈstent/ *n.* 程度；限度

⑥ capacity /kəˈpæsətɪ/ *n.* 容量；容积

⑦ distinctive /dɪˈstɪŋktɪv/ *adj.* 独特的；特别的

⑧ prodigious /prəˈdɪdʒəs/ *adj.* 巨大的；伟大的

⑨ distinguished /dɪˈstɪŋgwɪʃt/ *adj.* 卓越的；杰出的

⑩ admiration /ˌædməˈreɪʃn/ *n.* 钦佩；赞赏

枕戈待旦

Maintain Combat Readiness

 导入语　Lead-in

枕戈待旦,出自《晋书·刘琨传》:"吾枕戈待旦,志枭逆虏,常恐祖生先吾著鞭。"说的是西晋时期有两位有名的将军,一位叫刘琨,另一位叫祖逖,他们都是志向远大的青年;两人相交甚厚,常同床共寝,闻鸡起舞。后来,刘琨听说祖逖带兵打仗,颇受重用,很是

感慨。于是,他给亲朋写信说:"我头枕武器以待天亮,立志扫平敌寇,只是常常担心祖逖抢在我的前面。"意思是说,时刻警惕,准备作战,连睡觉时也不放松戒备,严阵以待。因此,后人便把刘琨所说的"枕戈待旦"作为成语,沿用至今。

 文化剪影 Cultural Outline

A letter expressed Liu Kun's eagerness to kill the enemy, serve the country and make **contributions**①, so that the story has been passed on by later generations. Then the idiom of Maintaining **Combat**② Readiness was used gradually, and the story behind of it is also admirable.

一封家书道出了刘琨杀敌报国、建功立业的急切心情,因此被后世代代传颂。后来,枕戈待旦被人们当作成语使用,而成语背后的故事也令人钦佩。

Liu Kun's **determination**③ to kill the enemy and serve the country at any time not only shows his loyalty and love for his country, but also reflects the heroism of ancient Chinese people with **lofty**④ ideals who went through fire and water for the national interest.

刘琨时刻准备杀敌报国的决心既表现了他对祖国的忠诚与热爱,又反映出中国古代仁人志士为了国家利益而赴汤蹈火的豪迈气概。

In today's view, the national spirit shown in this idiom story of Maintaining Combat Readiness still has a strong sense of **responsibility**⑤ and mission of the times. That kind of **intense**⑥ **patriotic**⑦ enthusiasm is something we should learn and hold in **esteem**⑧.

在今天看来,枕戈待旦这个成语故事中展现的民族精神依然体现出较强的时代责任感与使命感,这种强烈的爱国热情值得我们学习和推崇。

佳句点睛　Punchlines

1. The idiom of Maintaining Combat Readiness shows a strong sense of national spirit.

枕戈待旦这个成语体现了一种强烈的民族精神。

2. Liu Kun **resolved**⑨ to dedicate himself to serving the country.

刘琨决心献身报效自己的国家。

3. How many people of lofty ideals would go through fire and water for the national interest.

多少仁人志士为了国家利益赴汤蹈火。

情景对话　Situational Dialogue

A: Can you tell us what we learnt last Chinese class, Anna?

B: Yes, I can. We learned an idiom of "Maintain Combat Readiness".

A: Very good. So can you tell us the idiom story?

B: Sure. In the Western Jin Dynasty, there were two young men, one of them was Zu Ti, and the other was Liu Kun. Both of them were men with lofty ideals, and they were fond of practicing Wushu to keep fit to serve for the country. The idiom is about what happened to them.

119

A: OK, thank you. Is there anyone else to add? Wang Guo, please.

C: Later, after they departed, Zu Ti went to war with his troops. Deeply moved by the patriotic passion of Zu Ti, Liu Kun was determined to devote himself to his motherland. Once he wrote to his family, "At the time when the country is in danger, I would sleep with my head pillowed on a **spear**⑩ till the daybreak..."

A: Excellent!

A: 安娜，你能告诉大家上节中文课上我们学了什么内容吗？

B: 好的。我们学习了一个成语叫"枕戈待旦"。

A: 很好。你能给我们讲讲这个成语故事吗？

B: 当然可以。西晋时期，有两位年轻人。一位叫祖逖，另一位叫刘琨，他们俩都是有志青年，而且都喜欢练武健身，决心报效祖国。这个成语就跟他们俩有关。

A: 好的，谢谢你。还有人要做补充吗？王果，请说。

C: 后来，他们分开之后，祖逖带兵打仗。刘琨被祖逖的爱国热情深深地打动，也决心报效祖国。有一次，他在给家人的信中写道："在国家危难时刻，我时常整夜枕着兵器睡觉……"

A: 太棒了！

生词注解 Notes

① contribution /ˌkɒntrɪˈbjuːʃn/ *n.* 贡献

② combat /ˈkɒmbæt/ *vt.* 防止；抑制

③ determination /dɪˌtɜːmɪˈneɪʃn/ *n.* 决心；果断

④ lofty /ˈlɒftɪ/ *adj.* 崇高的；高尚的

⑤ responsibility /rɪˌspɒnsəˈbɪlətɪ/ *n.* 责任；职责

⑥ intense /ɪnˈtens/ *adj.* 强烈的；非常的

⑦ patriotic /ˌpeɪtrɪˈɒtɪk/ *adj.* 爱国的

⑧ esteem /ɪˈstiːm/ *n.* 尊重；敬重

⑨ resolve /rɪˈzɒlv/ *v.* 坚决；决心

⑩ spear /spɪə(r)/ *n.* 长矛；嫩枝

卧薪尝胆

Sleep on the Brushwood and Taste the Gall

导入语　Lead-in

卧薪尝胆的典故出自《史记·越王勾践世家》："越王勾践反国,乃苦身焦思,置胆于坐,坐卧即仰胆,饮食亦尝胆也。"讲的是春秋时期的越王勾践为了使自己铭记曾受的耻辱,激发斗志,在卧榻之侧挂上苦胆,每日尝一口胆汁,借此刻苦自励、发愤图强,最终完成了光复大业。后人对他这种"苦心人,天不负,卧薪尝胆,三千越甲可吞吴"的忍辱负重的豪迈气概进行了积极评价。卧薪尝胆原指越国国王勾践励精图治、以图复国的事迹,后演变为成语。

文化剪影　Cultural Outline

In the long history and culture of China over thousands of years, the story of Sleep on the Brushwood and Taste the Gall has been enriched by different literary works, and its idiom has become a household word, which has been widely circulated.

在中国几千年的历史文化长河中,卧薪尝胆的故事不断被各种文学作品加以丰富,该成语也变得家喻户晓,广为流传。

The story of Sleep on the Brushwood and Taste the Gall shows a kind of **perseverance**① and **indomitable**② spirit, which has a profound historical **vicissitudes**③ and philosophy of life. The spirit of enduring self-imposed hardships has also become the essence of traditional Chinese culture and passed down.

卧薪尝胆的故事体现了一种坚忍不拔、百折不挠的精神,蕴含厚重的历史沧桑感与深刻的人生哲理。卧薪尝胆的精神也作为中国传统文化的精华而流传下来。

The story of Goujian, King of Yue, who had a unique life experience in the history of Chinese emperors, has become a hero and a model for all of the Chinese people, and left behind a precious spiritual wealth for the great Chinese nation.

越王勾践,作为中国帝王史上拥有奇特人生经历的一代王者,已经成为历代华夏儿女的英雄榜样,也为伟大的中华民族留下了宝贵的精神财富。

佳句点睛　Punchlines

1. The story of Sleep on the Brushwood and Taste the Gall reflects a national spirit of perseverance and **tenacity**④.

卧薪尝胆的故事体现了一种坚忍不拔和不屈不挠的民族精神。

2. Goujian, King of Yue, had an extraordinary spirit and will.

越王勾践拥有超人的精神和意志。

3. The story of Sleep on the Brushwood and Taste the Gall is known as the classic in the history of Chinese civilization over thousands of years.

卧薪尝胆的故事被称为中国几千年文明史中的经典。

情景对话　Situational Dialogue

A: Lingling, who is the ancient person you admire most?

B: Well, I think I admire Hua Mulan most. What about you?

A: Gou Jian, King of Yue.

B: Why? Can you tell me more?

A: Sure. In the Spring and Autumn Period of China, there was a war between the states of Wu and Yue. Finally, Wu defeated Yue.

Gou Jian, King of Yue, was caught and **humiliated**⑤ in the State of Wu. Many years later, he was set free. After getting home, he began to plan his **revenge**⑥. In order to make himself tougher he slept on the brushwood and tasted **gall bladder**⑦ every day. At the same time, he **administered**⑧ his state carefully. After a few years, his country became strong. Then Gou Jian took advantage of an opportunity to wipe out the State of Wu.

B: Gou Jian had such a strong will that he could be the winner.

A: Yeah. That's why I like him.

A: 玲玲，你最敬佩的古代人物是谁？

B: 我最敬佩花木兰了！你呢？

A: 越王勾践。

B: 为什么？能给我讲讲吗？

A: 没问题。在中国的春秋时期，吴国和越国之间开战，最后以越国战败而告终。越王勾践被俘虏并且在吴国受尽了屈辱。多年以后，勾践被放回越国。归国后他就开始计划复仇。每晚他睡柴草、尝苦胆，以便激励自己；同时精心治理国家。几年后，越国又变得强大起来。后来，勾践抓住机会一举消灭了吴国。

B: 勾践具有坚强的意志，所以才成了赢家。

A: 是呀，这也是我喜欢他的原因。

 生词注解 Notes

① perseverance /ˌpɜːsəˈvɪərəns/ *n.* 毅力；韧性

② indomitable /ɪnˈdɒmɪtəbl/ *adj.* 不屈不挠的；勇敢坚定的

③ vicissitude /vɪˈsɪsɪtjuːd/ *n.* 兴衰；枯荣

④ tenacity /təˈnæsəti/ *n.* 韧性；坚忍不拔

⑤ humiliate /hjuːˈmɪlieɪt/ *vt.* 羞辱；使……丧失尊严

⑥ revenge /rɪˈvendʒ/ *n.* 报复；报仇

⑦ gall bladder /ˈɡɔːl blædə(r)/ *n.* 胆囊；苦胆

⑧ administer /ədˈmɪnɪstə(r)/ *vt.* 治理；掌管

沉鱼落雁

Make Fish Sink and Wild Geese Alight

导入语 Lead-in

沉鱼落雁,出自庄子的《齐物论》:"毛嫱、丽姬,人之所美也;鱼见之深入,鸟见之高飞,麋鹿见之决骤,四者孰知天下之正色哉?"意思是说,鱼

见之沉入水底,雁见之降落沙洲。庄子的原意是说,美是相对的,美与丑并没有统一的固定标准。沉鱼落雁后来逐渐引申为成语使用,其意思也发生了变化,泛指女子容貌惊艳。中国人习惯把"沉鱼落雁"和"闭月羞花"同时使用,分别指中国历史上的四大美女:西施、王昭君、貂蝉和杨贵妃,她们享有"闭月羞花之貌,沉鱼落雁之容"的美名。

 文化剪影 Cultural Outline

The idiom of Make Fish Sink and Wild Geese Alight has **undergone**① **fundamental**② changes **in terms of**③ content and meaning, which has become a well-known **compliment**④ to the appearances of women.

成语沉鱼落雁在含义上产生了根本的变化,从而变成了大家熟知的对女子容貌的赞美之辞。

The idiom of Make Fish Sink and Wild Geese Alight has become the embodiment and **synonym**⑤ of beauty, and it is a literary creation of beautiful things from romantic ancient people and reflects an **implicit**⑥ beauty in the expression of ancient Chinese literature.

沉鱼落雁成为了美的化身和代名词,它是古人对美好事物进行的浪漫主义的文学创作,体现了中国古代文学表达的一种含蓄之美。

The ancient Chinese **literati**⑦ used their intelligence and romantic imagination to carry out artistic processing in literature, and reflected the female's **incomparable**⑧ beauty by the description of animals' reaction to beautiful women.

中国古代文人发挥聪明才智和浪漫想象进行文学上的艺术加工,通过描述自然界中的动物对美丽女子的反应来衬托女性无与伦比的美貌。

佳句点睛　Punchlines

1. The idiom of Make Fish Sink and Wild Geese Alight reflects an implicit beauty in the expression of ancient Chinese literature.
沉鱼落雁体现了中国古代文学表达的含蓄美。

2. Xishi's appearance made the fish sink for shame while Zhaojun's let the wild geese alight.
西施有沉鱼之貌，昭君有落雁之容。

3. Nowadays, the idiom of Making Fish Sink and Wild Geese Alight means the synonym of beauty.
如今，沉鱼落雁这个成语成为美的代名词。

情景对话　Situational Dialogue

A: Have you seen the latest movie? The actress is so **gorgeous**①.

B: Yes, I have. I'd prefer to use the Chinese idiom "Chen Yu Luo Yan" to describe her beauty.

A: Is that a compliment?

B: Of course. "Chen Yu" denotes Xishi, and "Luo Yan" refers to Wang Zhaojun. Both of them were beauties. It is said that Xishi went to the creek to wash clothes every day, and when the fish in the creek saw her, they would be lost in her beauty, forget to swim and sink to the bottom of the creek. As a result, Xishi had the fame of "the beauty that made the fish sink".

A: An interesting story. Then I think Wang Zhaojun had the beauty that made the wild geese fall out of the sky.

B: That's right.

A: 你看最新的电影了吗？女主角简直太美了！

B: 我看了。我更喜欢用中国成语"沉鱼落雁"来形容她的美。

A: 那是赞美的话吗？

B: 当然是了。"沉鱼"指的是西施，"落雁"指的是昭君。她们都是美女。据说西施每天去河边洗衣服，水里的鱼儿见了她的美貌都不知游动，以致沉入水底。因此，西施就有了"沉鱼之貌"的美名。

A: 这个故事有意思。那么，我想昭君就有了落雁之美。

B: 说得对。

生词注解 Notes

① undergo /ˌʌndəˈɡəʊ/ vt. 经历；经受（变化、不快的事等）

② fundamental /ˌfʌndəˈmentl/ adj. 根本的；基本的

③ in terms of 谈及；就……而言

④ compliment /ˈkɒmplɪmənt/ n. 赞扬；称赞

⑤ synonym /ˈsɪnənɪm/ n. 同义词

⑥ implicit /ɪmˈplɪsɪt/ adj. 含蓄的；不直接言明的

⑦ literati /ˌlɪtəˈrɑːtɪ/ *n.* 文人学士

⑧ incomparable /ɪnˈkɒmprəbl/ *adj.* 不可比拟的；无比的

⑨ gorgeous /ˈɡɔːdʒəs/ *adj.* 非常漂亮的；美丽动人的

滥竽充数

Make up the Number

 导入语 Lead-in

滥竽充数,出自《韩非子·内储说上》:"齐宣王使人吹竽,必三百人。南郭处士请为王吹竽,宣王说之,食以数百人。宣王死,湣王立,好一一听之,处士逃。"讲的是战国时期,齐宣王非常喜欢听吹竽合奏,不会吹竽的南郭先生想办法混进了乐队,以得到丰厚的报酬。齐宣王去世后,齐湣王继承王位,他喜欢听吹竽独奏,南郭先生得知后便逃之夭夭。后来,人们根据这个寓言故事概括出了"滥竽充数"这一成语,比喻没有真才实学的人混在内行人中以次充好。有时也用作自谦之辞。

文化剪影 Cultural Outline

The story of Make up the Number is interesting and vividly the behavior of Mr. Nanguo in the story has made a deep impression on people. After some evolution, the idiom about the story has been widely used by people.

滥竽充数这个故事既有趣又生动,尤其是南郭先生的一系列行为给人留下了深刻的印象。几经演变后,这个故事就成了一个被人们广泛使用的成语。

The story of Make up the Number **satirizes**① people as **ignorant**② as Mr. Nanguo, showing that only people with **genuine**③ talent can **stand**④ the test of practice.

滥竽充数这个成语讽刺了像南郭先生一样不学无术的人,说明了唯有真才实学才能经得起实践的考验。

Abstract⑤ truth is contained in a humorous and vivid story, which has a certain artistic quality of language and also has brought useful reference to people.

寓抽象的道理于幽默生动的故事之中,既具有一定的语言艺术性,又给人们带来了有益的借鉴。

 佳句点睛 Punchlines

1. The idiom of Make up the Number is used to sneer at someone who **disguises**© himself as a profession in a certain field.

滥竽充数这个成语用来讽刺那些在某一领域没有真实才干的人。

2. Only people with genuine talent who can stand the test of practice.

唯有真才实学才能经得起实践的考验。

3. The story of Make up the Number has brought people helpful reference.

滥竽充数的故事给人们带来了有益的借鉴。

 情景对话 Situational Dialogue

A: Hi, Jack. How was the performance yesterday?

B: Hi, Eric. It was terrible.

A: I'm sorry to hear that. What's wrong?

B: Because Ben knew nothing about the performance.

A: It sounds like he's another Mr. Nanguo.

B: What does that mean?

A: Long long ago, the King of Qi was very fond of listening to the Yu **ensembles**⑦. He often got three hundred Yu players to form a grand music. A man named Nanguo heard about that and managed to join in the band, even though he wasn't good at playing the instrument at all. Later when the King died, his son became the new ruler who also liked the music played on the Yu. But he preferred **solos**⑧. As soon as he got the news, Nanguo **sneaked**⑨ away as fast as he could.

B: I see. He disguised himself as a musician.

A: Yes, but he was a **layman**⑩ indeed.

A: 你好,杰克。昨天的表演怎么样?

B: 你好,埃里克。昨天的表演糟透了。

A: 真是遗憾! 怎么回事?

B: 因为本对表演一无所知。

A: 听上去他就像是另一位南郭先生。

B: 此话何意?

A: 很久以前,齐国的国王很喜欢听三百人的吹竽合奏。有一位南郭先生尽管不擅长吹竽,但也设法混进了乐队,以便得到丰厚的报酬。后来,国王去世,他的儿子继承了王位。他也喜欢听竽,但他只喜欢听独奏。南郭先生得知消息后便赶紧逃跑了。

B: 我明白了,他是假冒乐师。

A: 是的,但他的确是个门外汉。

生词注解 Notes

① satirize /ˈsætəraɪz/　vt. 讽刺；讥讽

② ignorant /ˈɪɡnərənt/　adj. 不了解的；无知的

③ genuine /ˈdʒenjuɪn/　adj. 真正的；正宗的

④ stand /stænd/　vt. 经受；承受

⑤ abstract /ˈæbstrækt/　adj. 抽象的

⑥ disguise /dɪsˈɡaɪz/　vt. 假扮；伪装

⑦ ensemble /ɒnˈsɒmbl/　n. 乐团；剧团

⑧ solo /ˈsəʊləʊ/　n. 独奏；独唱

⑨ sneak /sniːk/　v. 偷偷地走；溜

⑩ layman /ˈleɪmən/　n. 外行；门外汉

画蛇添足

Draw a Snake and Add Feet to It

 导入语 Lead-in

画蛇添足，源自《战国策·齐策二》："楚有祠者，赐其舍人卮酒，舍人相谓曰：'数人饮之不足，一人饮之有余，请画地为蛇，先成者饮酒。'一人蛇先成，引酒且饮之，乃左手持卮，右手画蛇曰：'吾能为之足。'未成，一人之蛇成，夺其卮曰：'蛇固无足，子安能为之足？'遂饮其酒。为蛇足者，终亡其酒。"讲的是楚国有一家人不知怎么分配祭祖的酒，于是便想了一个办法：谁画蛇又快又好，就让谁喝酒。有一个人最先画完，但他却给蛇添上了脚，结果错失了好酒。后来，人们根据这个故事引申出了"画蛇添足"这个成语，比喻做了多余的事，不但无益，反而不宜，也比喻虚构事实，无中生有。这个成语同时也告

诫人们做事要实事求是，不要自作聪明，否则会弄巧成拙，适得其反。

文化剪影　Cultural Outline

With the constant development and changes in people's language habits and lifestyles, the story of Draw a Snake and Add Feet to It has also changed in its expression. The form of its **concise**① idiom has been gradually loved and widely used by people.

随着人们语言习惯、生活方式的不断发展与变化，画蛇添足的故事在表达方式上也随之改变。简洁的成语形式逐渐被人们喜爱，并得以广泛使用。

It is recorded in ***The Stratagems***② of the Warring States, "The man who drew a snake and added feet to it didn't get the good wine." This story illustrates that people who are too smart for their own good are often too blindly **optimistic**③ and will eventually lead to failure.

《战国策》中记载："为蛇足者，终亡其酒。"这个故事说明了自作聪明的人往往过于盲目乐观，最终会导致失败的结局。

Draw a Snake and Add Feet to It and **Outsmarting**④ Oneself can mean that you think you have done well, but in fact you have done badly. However, the former **focuses on**⑤ doing **superfluous**⑥ things while the latter stresses on trying to do better.

画蛇添足和弄巧成拙都可表示自以为做得好，结果坏了事。但是，画蛇添足偏重于做多余之事，弄巧成拙偏重于想做得好些。

佳句点睛　Punchlines

1. Those who are blindly optimistic will fail in the end.
那些盲目乐观的人最终会失败。

2. The story of Draw a Snake and Add Feet to It tells us that a smart aleck tends to make things worse.
画蛇添足这个故事告诉我们，自作聪明的人往往会弄巧成拙。

3. The beauty of lily lies in its purity, not in its gorgeousness. After being gilt, it has no former pure beauty, just like drawing a snake and adding feet to it.
百合花的美在于清纯而不在于华丽，镀金之后反而没有之前的清纯丽质，就像画蛇添足一样。

情景对话　Situational Dialogue

A: Happy New Year, Emma.
B: Happy New Year, Julie.
A: It's the year of snake. Do you know anything about snake?
B: I just learned an idiom about it yesterday. Er, I can't remember it right now.

A: Draw a Snake and Add Feet to It?

B: Yes, that's it. Do you know the story about this idiom?

A: Yeah. A man in the State of Chu was offering a **sacrifice**[7] to his ancestors. After the ceremony, the man gave a pot of wine to his servants; the servants thought that there was not enough for all of them, and decided to each draw a picture of snake. The one who finished firstly would get the wine. One of them drew rapidly, seeing that the others were still busy drawing, he added feet to the snake. At this moment, another man finished, he **snatched**[8] the pot and said, "A snake doesn't have feet, how can you add them to it?"

B: It's really an amusing story.

A: 新年快乐,爱玛。

B: 新年快乐,朱莉。

A: 今年是蛇年。你知道关于蛇的知识吗?

B: 我昨天刚学了一个关于蛇的成语,可现在却想不起来了。

A: 是画蛇添足吗?

B: 是,就是这个。你知道这个成语故事吗?

A: 我知道。楚国有个人祭完祖先之后,将祭祀用的一壶酒赏给仆人们喝。仆人们觉得一壶酒不够分,于是想出了一个办法:谁能快速画好一条蛇,这壶酒就归谁。有个人很快就画好了,他看其他人仍在继续画,于是就给蛇画了脚。正在这时,另一个人也完成了,他一把抓过酒壶说道:"蛇根本没有脚,你怎么能给它画脚呢?"

B: 这个故事真有趣。

生词注解 Notes

① concise /kənˈsaɪs/ *adj.* 简明的；简洁的

② stratagem /ˈstrætədʒəm/ *n.* (为取胜或迷惑对手的)计策；计谋

③ optimistic /ˌɒptɪˈmɪstɪk/ *adj.* 乐观的；乐观主义的

④ outsmart /ˌaʊtˈsmɑːt/ *vt.* 智取；用计谋打败

⑤ focus on 专注于……；集中于……

⑥ superfluous /suːˈpɜːfluəs/ *adj.* 多余的；不必要的

⑦ sacrifice /ˈsækrɪfaɪs/ *n.* 祭献；祭祀

⑧ snatch /snætʃ/ *vt.* 一把抓起；一下夺过

按图索骥

Look for a Steed by Its Picture

导入语 Lead-in

据明代杨慎的《艺林伐山·卷七》记载，春秋时期，秦国著名的相马专家孙阳因善识马而被人们称为"伯乐"，他根据自己的经验写了《相马经》。他的儿子很想把相马的绝技学到手，于是就熟读《相马经》，并根据书上的标准选出了"千里马"——一只癞蛤蟆，他回家向父亲报喜，伯乐看后哭笑不得。伯乐的儿子因不得相马术的要领，只知道生搬硬套，结果闹出了笑话。这就是按图索骥的故事。按图索骥是指按照图像去寻找好马，比喻做事拘泥于教条，墨守成规，现在也指顺着线索去寻找。

文化剪影 Cultural Outline

In the long **course**① of civilization development, the story of Look for a **Steed**② by Its Picture has been passed on and on. To make it easier to remember, people **summarized**③ the story into an idiom, which has been passed down to this day.

在漫长的文明发展历程中,按图索骥的故事不断流传。为了便于记忆,人们将这个故事内容概括为成语,流传至今。

The story of Look for a Steed by Its Picture is rich in interest and philosophy, which carries the unique values of the Chinese nation and still has educational significance nowadays.

按图索骥这个故事富有趣味性,又饱含哲理性,承载着中华民族特有的价值观念,至今仍具有教育意义。

In ancient times, horses were **indispensable**④ to people, which carried many important tasks in transportation and **military**⑤ affairs. So knowing how to judge a horse's worth by its appearance was a **crucial**⑥ skill.

在古代,马匹对人们来说不可或缺,在运输、军事中承载着多种重任,因此相马是一项至关重要的技能。

 佳句点睛　Punchlines

1. The story of Look for a Steed by Its Picture still has educational significance nowadays.

按图索骥的故事至今仍有教育意义。

2. The mistake of Look for a Steed by Its Picture is that the theory is divorced from reality and **dogmatism**⑦.

按图索骥的错误之处在于理论脱离实际和教条主义。

3. The story of Look for a Steed by Its Picture is rich in interest and philosophy.

按图索骥的故事既富有趣味性，又饱含哲理性。

 情景对话　Situational Dialogue

A: Jenny, take care of your brother, please. I'm busy right now.

B: OK, mom.

C: Jenny, I wanna go out to play.

B: No. It's raining. How about telling a story?

C: Yes. I love that.

B: During the Spring and Autumn Period of China, there was a man named Sun Yang. He was an expert in looking at horses and judging their worth. He wrote a book entitled *Xiang Ma Jing* (*Classics of Identifying the Thoroughbred*), based on his experiences and knowledge. Sun Yang had a son, who thought it easy to **appraise**⑧ horses after reading the book, so he took the book with him to look for fine horses. At first, he searched according to the pictures in the book and got nothing. Then he found that a toad agreed with the characteristics of a fine horse described in the book. So he happily took the toad back home.

C: The son was so funny.

B: Yeah. But the story is also **philosophical**⑨.

A: 珍妮,照顾一下弟弟。我现在很忙。

B: 好的,妈妈。

C: 珍妮,我想出去玩。

B: 不行,正下着雨呢。讲故事怎么样?

C: 好啊,我喜欢。

B: 在中国的春秋时期,有一位名叫孙阳的人擅长相马,他根据自己相马的经验和知识写了一本书,书名叫《相马经》。孙阳有个儿子,他看了父亲的书后,以为相马很容易,于是就拿着书到处找好马。起初,他按照书上所绘的图形去找马,一无所获。然后又按照书中所写的特征去找,发现有只癞蛤蟆很像书中所说的好马的特征,于是便高兴地把癞蛤蟆带回了家。

C: 这个儿子真好笑!

B: 是呀。不过,这个故事也很有哲理性。

生词注解 Notes

① course /kɔːs/　*n.* 进程；过程

② steed /stiːd/　*n.* 骏马；战马

③ summarize /ˈsʌməraɪz/　*vt.* 总结；概括

④ indispensable /ˌɪndɪˈspensəbl/　*adj.* 不可或缺的；必不可少的

⑤ military /ˈmɪlətri/　*adj.* 军事的；军队的

⑥ crucial /ˈkruːʃl/　*adj.* 至关重要的；关键性的

⑦ dogmatism /ˈdɒɡmətɪzəm/　*n.* 教条主义；独断

⑧ appraise /əˈpreɪz/　*vt.* 估量；估价

⑨ philosophical /ˌfɪləˈsɒfɪkl/　*adj.* 哲理性的；哲学的

揠苗助长

Uproot Seedlings to Spur Growth

 导入语　Lead-in

揠苗助长,出自《孟子·公孙丑上》,讲的是古时候有个宋国人,他急切期盼禾苗长高,就想了一个办法,去田里把禾苗一个个拔高,虽十分疲劳,但却心满意足。回到家里后,他告诉了家人,他的儿子知道后急忙跑到田里去查看,结果发现禾苗早已干枯了。这个故事后来被人们概括成了成语"揠苗助长",也称为"拔苗助长"。这则成语的意思是把禾苗拔起,以帮助其生长。比喻违反事物发展的客观规律,急于求成,反而会弄巧成拙、适得其反。

 文化剪影　Cultural Outline

The story of **Uproot**① Seedlings to **Spur**② Growth is lively and interesting, which outlines a funny **figure**③ who lived in ancient times and inspires people with wisdom. Gradually, the story was **refined**④ into a familiar idiom.

揠苗助长的故事生动有趣,勾勒出了一个可笑的古人形象,并给人以智慧的启迪,后来逐渐精炼成了大家耳熟能详的成语。

The story of Uproot Seedlings to Spur Growth tells people that everything has its own laws of development. Once they go against the laws of nature, people will be punished. The story also reflects the philosophical features of ancient traditional culture.

揠苗助长的故事告诉人们万事万物都有其自身的发展规律,一旦违背了自然规律,就会受到惩罚。这个故事也反映了古代传统文化的哲学特点。

Farming culture is one of the characteristics of traditional Chinese culture. It calls for gradual and orderly progress during the farming season, and then man can live in a harmony with nature.

农耕文化是中国传统文化的特点之一,它要求不违农时、循序渐进,从而达到人与自然的和谐统一。

佳句点睛　Punchlines

1. The story of Uproot Seedlings to Spur Growth **outlines**⑤ a funny figure who lived in ancient times.

握苗助长的故事勾勒出一个可笑的古人形象。

2. Once they go against the laws of nature, people will be surely punished **accordingly**⑥.

人一旦违背了自然规律，就必然会受到相应的惩罚。

3. The story of Uproot Seedlings to Spur Growth is of certain philosophical significance.

握苗助长的故事具有一定的哲学意义。

情景对话　Situational Dialogue

A: I love Chinese culture very much. They're so interesting.

B: For example?

A: Even an idiom has its own story. Now I'll tell you a funny story, can you name its idiom?

B: Why don't you have a try?

A: There was a farmer in the State of Song who had an impatient **disposition**⑦. Every day he longed for the seedlings in the field to grow tall and strong quickly, but the seedlings didn't grow as quickly as he hoped. One day he hit upon a good idea. He went to the field and pulled each seedling up a little bit from the soil. When he got home happily, he told his son about the **brilliant**⑧ method. His son hurried to the field and found that the seedlings had all started to **wither**⑨.

B: Er, Uproot Seedlings to Spur Growth.

A: You got it.

A: 我太喜欢中国文化了,它们很有意思。

B: 比如说?

A: 每个成语都包含一个故事。我来给你讲个有趣的故事,看看你能不能说出它对应的成语。

B: 何不试一下呢!

A: 宋国有位急性子的农夫,他每天都盼望着田里的禾苗茁壮生长。可是,禾苗并没有像他所希望的那样飞快生长。一天,他想出了一个好办法。他来到田里,把禾苗一颗一颗从泥土里往上拔高了一些。他高兴地回到家里,并把这个好办法告诉了儿子。他的儿子急忙跑到田里去看,结果禾苗全都枯萎了。

B: 呃,揠苗助长。

A: 答对了!

生词注解 Notes

① uproot /ˌʌpˈruːt/ vt. 根除;连根拔起

② spur /spɜː(r)/ vt. 刺激；促进

③ figure /ˈfɪɡə(r)/ n. 重要人物；身影

④ refine /rɪˈfaɪn/ vt. 改进；使……精练

⑤ outline /ˈaʊtlaɪn/ vt. 概述；映衬出……的轮廓

⑥ accordingly /əˈkɔːdɪŋli/ adv. 因此；相应地

⑦ disposition /ˌdɪspəˈzɪʃn/ n. 性格；性情

⑧ brilliant /ˈbrɪliənt/ adj. 绝妙的；非常棒的

⑨ wither /ˈwɪðə(r)/ v. 枯萎；凋谢

亡羊补牢

Mend the Fold after the Sheep Is Lost

  导入语 Lead-in

亡羊补牢,出自《战国策·楚策》:"见兔而顾犬,未为晚也;亡羊而补牢,未为迟也。"说的是战国时期,楚襄王荒淫无度,执迷不悟,将劝谏的大臣庄辛赶出楚国。秦国趁此征伐,很快占领了楚国国都。楚襄王后悔不已,派人请回庄辛,庄辛说:"见兔而顾犬,未为晚也;亡羊则补牢,未为迟也。"他鼓励楚襄王励精图治,重整旗鼓。"亡羊补牢"这个成语便由此而来,意思是羊丢失了再去修补羊圈,还不算晚。比喻事情出了差错后,要马上采取防范措施,以免节外生枝再出问题。

文化剪影　Cultural Outline

Zhuang Xin took the story of Mend the **Fold**① after the Sheep Is Lost as an example of **admonishing**② the king of Chu. He finally succeeded in persuading the king. Later, mending the fold after the sheep is lost has become a household idiom in traditional Chinese culture.

庄辛把亡羊补牢作为劝谏楚王的一个例证,不仅成功说服了楚王,也使"亡羊补牢"成为了中国传统文化中一个家喻户晓的成语。

The story of Mend the Fold after the Sheep Is Lost shows people the **eloquent**③ power of the wise minister Zhuang Xin to move people's hearts and also represents his **concern**④ for the country and the people. So Zhuang Xin is regarded as a model of **patriotism**⑤.

亡羊补牢的故事让人们看到了贤臣庄辛打动人心的雄辩之力,更体现了他的忧国忧民之心。所以,庄辛被视为爱国主义的典范。

Zhuang Xin encouraged the King of Chu to regroup by telling the story of how to mend the lost battle. His **superb**⑥ skills of expression showed the charm of language and the wisdom of debate.

庄辛借用故事来鼓励楚王重整旗鼓,他高超的表达技巧展现了语言的魅力和辩论的智慧。

 佳句点睛　Punchlines

1. Mending the Fold after the Sheep Is Lost is a household idiom in traditional Chinese culture.

亡羊补牢是中国传统文化中一个家喻户晓的成语。

2. Zhuang Xin was a loyal minister who cared about his country and the people.

庄辛是一位忧国忧民的忠臣。

3. Zhuang Xin successfully **remonstrated**[7] with the king of Chu with excellent language skills.

庄辛利用高超的语言技巧成功劝谏了楚王。

 情景对话　Situational Dialogue

A: Hi, Paul. You looked so upset.

B: Yeah. I failed the final match.

A: I'm so sorry. Don't worry about that. It's not too late if you mend the fold when you find a sheep is lost.

B: What's that meaning?

A: Well, that's an old Chinese story. There was a shepherd who kept several sheep. One morning he discovered that one of his sheep was lost. It turned out that a wolf had stolen it at night through a hole in the fold. His neighbor suggested him mending the fold, but he thought it was not necessary to do that because the sheep was already lost. The next morning, another sheep missed once again. At this time, the shepherd regretted not taking the neighbor's advice. So he **plugged**® the hole to secure the fold immediately. From then on, no more sheep has been stolen by the wolf.

B: Thank you for telling the story, Jane. I think I should prepare for the next match.

A: My pleasure. Good luck!

B: Good luck!

A: 你好,保罗。你看起来不开心啊!

B: 是的。我在决赛中失利了。

A: 真是遗憾! 不过别担心,亡羊补牢,还不算太晚。

B: 此话何意?

A: 嗯,这是一个古老的中国故事。有个人养了几只羊,一天早上他发现羊少了一只。原来羊圈破了个窟窿,夜里狼从窟窿里把羊叼走了。邻居劝他修补羊圈,他却认为羊已经丢了,没必要去修。第二天早上,又有一只羊不见了。直到这时,他才后悔没有听邻居的劝告,于是赶紧修补羊圈上的窟窿。从此以后,他的羊再也没被狼叼走过。

B: 谢谢你告诉这个故事,简。我想我应该备战下次的比赛了。

A: 不客气。祝你好运!

B: 祝你好运！

生词注解 Notes

① fold /fəʊld/ *n.* 羊栏；羊圈

② admonish /ədˈmɒnɪʃ/ *vt.* 告诫；劝告

③ eloquent /ˈeləkwənt/ *adj.* 雄辩的；有口才的

④ concern /kənˈsɜːn/ *n.* 担忧；关心

⑤ patriotism /ˈpeɪtrɪətɪzəm/ *n.* 爱国主义；爱国精神

⑥ superb /suːˈpɜːb/ *adj.* 一流的；极好的

⑦ remonstrate /ˈremənstreɪt/ *vt.* 抗议；抱怨

⑧ plug /plʌɡ/ *vt.* 堵塞；封堵

邯郸学步

Imitate to Walk in Handan

导入语 Lead-in

邯郸学步,也作"学步邯郸",出自《庄子·秋水》:"且子独不闻夫寿陵馀子之学行于邯郸与?未得国能,又失其故行矣,直匍匐而归耳。"说的是战国时期,燕国寿陵

有一位少年,他听说赵国邯郸人走路的姿势特别优美,就千里迢迢来到邯郸,学习当地人走路的姿势。结果,他不但没有学会,反而忘记了自己原来的走法,只好爬着回到了燕国。"邯郸学步"这个成语由此而来,用来比喻一味地模仿别人,不仅学不到别人的长处,反而把自己的优点和本领也丢掉了。

 文化剪影 Cultural Outline

The story of Imitate to Walk in Handan is humorous and interesting, which makes people think deeply. For thousands of years, this interesting story has been handed down to the present day, whose content has been gradually condensed into idioms, constantly **admonishing**① people.

邯郸学步的故事诙谐风趣，引人深思。几千年来，这个有趣的故事流传至今并逐渐被简练为成语，时刻告诫着人们。

The story of Imitate to Walk in Handan tells people in a **metaphorical**② way that if they **imitate**③ others blindly, they will lose themselves eventually. So people should learn to **proceed**④ from their own reality and overcome their shortcomings by learning others' strong points.

邯郸学步以隐喻的方式告诉人们，盲目地模仿别人最终会失去自我；要学会从自身实际出发，取人之长，补己之短。

The story of Imitate to Walk in Handan is **enduring**⑤ and of profound significance. Therefore, within the city of Handan, Hebei Province, there is a bridge named Xuebu (Learning to Walk) related to this idiom story. Beside the old bridge sits a stone carving that vividly **depicts**⑥ the story.

邯郸学步的故事经久不衰，意义深远，在河北省邯郸市还建有与此故事有关的学步桥。古桥旁边坐落着石雕,逼真地再现了这个故事。

佳句点睛 Punchlines

1. Imitate to Walk in Handan tells people profound truth by metaphor.

邯郸学步以隐喻的方式告诉人们深刻的道理。

2. People who blindly imitate others will eventually lose themselves.

一味模仿别人,最终会失去自我。

3. Imitate to Walk in Handan tells us that it is impossible to apply **mechanically**[⑦] and learning from **innovation**[⑧] is a good way to go.

邯郸学步告诉我们:生搬硬套是行不通的,要学会借鉴、创新。

情景对话 Situational Dialogue

A: Welcome to Handan. It's an old and beautiful city. Now what you can see is the famous scenic spot named Xuebu Bridge.

B: Thank you. Does it mean a small child learns to walk on this bridge?

A: Actually no. It's about an idiom. You know, Handan is the hometown of idioms.

B: Tell me about it, please.

A: In ancient times, Handan, capital of Zhao, was famous for people's graceful walking style. People in other places admired them very much. A young man of Yan traveled a long way to Handan to learn how to walk. However, it was easier said than done. No matter how hard he tried, he just couldn't walk the way the people in Handan did. What was worse, he even forgot his own way of walking. Finally, he had to crawl all the way back.

B: Gosh, what a poor man he was!

A: 欢迎来到邯郸！这是一座古老而美丽的城市。现在你看到的就是著名的景点——学步桥。

B: 谢谢！学步桥的意思是不是小孩在上面学走路？

A: 其实不是，它与一个成语有关，邯郸是成语之乡呢。

B: 请给我讲讲吧。

A: 古时候，赵国邯郸人以走路姿势优美而闻名，其他地方的人都很羡慕他们。有一位燕国的少年千里迢迢来到邯郸学习走路方式。可说起来容易做起来难。他怎么努力也学不会邯郸人走路的姿势。更糟糕的是，他连自己原来的走法也忘记了，最后只好爬着回燕国去。

B: 天哪，他真可怜！

生词注解 Notes

① admonish /ədˈmɒnɪʃ/ vt. 告诫；劝告

② metaphorical /ˌmetəˈfɒrɪkl/ adj. 隐喻的；含比喻的

③ imitate /ˈɪmɪteɪt/ vt. 模仿（某人的讲话、举止）

④ proceed /prəˈsiːd/ v. 继续做（或从事、进行）

⑤ enduring /ɪnˈdjʊərɪŋ/ adj. 持久的；耐久的

⑥ depict /dɪˈpɪkt/ vt. 描写；描述

⑦ mechanically /məˈkænɪklɪ/ adv. 机械地；呆板地

⑧ innovation /ˌɪnəˈveɪʃn/ n.（新事物、思想或方法的）创造；创新

讳疾忌医

Hide One's Sickness for Fear of Treatment

 导入语　Lead-in

讳疾忌医，源自《韩非子·喻老》，讲述了名医扁鹊几次谒见蔡桓公，都看出桓公身患疾病，而且一次比一次严重，但蔡桓公却不愿承认，也不肯就医，导致疾病由肌肤恶化到骨髓，最终因无法医治而身亡。后来，宋朝周敦颐在《周子通书·过》中记载："今人有过，不喜人规，如讳疾而忌医，宁灭其身而无悟也。"自此，"讳疾忌医"这个成语便被广泛使用，意思是指隐瞒疾病，害怕医治。比喻掩饰缺点和错误，不愿改正。

文化剪影　Cultural Outline

The story of Bian Que's exhortation to Marquis Huan of Cai to seek medical attention in a timely manner is memorable, and what it reveals is thought-provoking. After Zhou Dunyi of the Song Dynasty used the idiom of Hide One's Sickness for Fear of Treatment, it has spread and become popular until now.

扁鹊劝蔡桓公及时就医的故事令人印象深刻,它所揭示的道理发人深省。在宋朝的周敦颐使用"讳疾忌医"后,这个成语便由此流传开来并沿用至今。

Hide One's Sickness for Fear of Treatment tells people to face up to their shortcomings and mistakes, accept others' opinions modestly, and nip them in the bud. Otherwise, it will eventually bring dire **consequences**[1].

讳疾忌医告诉人们要正视自己的缺点和错误,虚心接受他人的意见,防患于未然。否则会带来不堪设想的后果。

Bian Que made **outstanding**[2] contributions to traditional Chinese medicine. He paid great attention to the prevention of diseases, believing that the disease can be **eliminated**[3] at the **initial**[4] stage by taking measures in advance. For a long time, he has been deeply loved by people for his superb medical skill and noble medical **ethics**[5].

扁鹊对中医学作出了卓越的贡献。他十分注重疾病的预防,认

为对疾病预先采取措施,可以把疾病消灭在初始阶段。一直以来,扁鹊因精湛的医术和高尚的医德而深受人们的爱戴。

 佳句点睛   Punchlines

1. If one person cannot face up to his shortcomings and mistakes, there will be unimaginable consequences in the end.

如果一个人不能正视自己的缺点和错误,最终会带来不堪设想的后果。

2. Bian Que has made outstanding contributions to traditional Chinese medicine.

扁鹊对中医学作出了卓越的贡献。

3. For thousands of years, Bian Que has been deeply loved by people for his excellent medical skills and noble medical ethics.

几千年来,扁鹊因精湛的医术和高尚的医德而深受人们的爱戴。

 情景对话   Situational Dialogue

A: Now, please look at the picture carefully, then tell me who they are. You, please.

B: They're Bian Que and Marquis Huan of Cai.

A: Good. Thank you. What happened between them?

B: Bian Que was a famous doctor. After seeing Marquis Huan of Cai, he told Marquis Huan of Cai that his illness had **intruded**⑥ into skin and needed to be treated immediately. But Marquis Huan of Cai thought he was in good health, so he **ignored**⑦ what the doctor said. Later, Bian Que persuaded him a few times, yet Marquis Huan of Cai had not said anything. Finally, Marquis Huan of Cai died of his illness.

A: Very good! You explained in great detail.

A: 现在请大家仔细看这张图片,告诉我图上的人分别是谁。你来回答。

B: 他们是扁鹊和蔡桓公。

A: 很好,谢谢!他们之间发生了什么事呢?

B: 名医扁鹊见到蔡桓公后,告诉蔡桓公他的疾病已侵入肌肤,需要赶紧治疗。而蔡桓公觉得自己很健康,不予理睬。后来,扁鹊又多次劝他诊治,蔡桓公依然无动于衷。最后,蔡桓公不治而亡。

A: 很好!你介绍得很详细。

生词注解 Notes

① consequence /ˈkɒnsɪkwəns/ n. 结果;后果

② outstanding /aʊtˈstændɪŋ/ adj. 杰出的;出色的

③ eliminate /ɪˈlɪmɪneɪt/ vt. 清除;消除

④ initial /ɪˈnɪʃl/ adj. 最初的；开始的

⑤ ethic /ˈeθɪk/ n. 道德准则；伦理标准

⑥ intrude /ɪnˈtruːd/ vt. 侵入；侵扰

⑦ ignore /ɪgˈnɔː(r)/ vt. 忽视；对……不予理会

掩耳盗铃

Cover the Ears to Steal the Bell

  导入语　Lead-in

掩耳盗铃,原为"掩耳盗钟",出自《吕氏春秋·自知》的一则寓言故事。本意为偷钟的人怕别人听见钟声捂住自己的耳朵,以为自己听不见别人也会听

不见。故事大意是,有一个人看见别人家院子里吊着一口精美的大钟,想把它偷走。由于钟太重背不动,因此他决定用槌子把钟砸碎再背回家。但他刚一动手,钟就响起来了。这个人急忙捂住自己的耳朵,以为别人也听不到响声了。后人就用"掩耳盗铃"这一成语来比喻明明掩盖不住的事情,却偏要想办法掩盖,结果只能自己骗自己。

文化剪影 Cultural Outline

The story of Cover the Ears to Steal the Bell is **ridiculous**① and stupid, and then it developed into an idiom. In ancient times, zhong was an instrument. With the changes of the times, which is **eliminated**② gradually, and bell is more common in daily life. So the idiom of Cover the Ears to Steal the Bell has been widely used.

掩耳盗铃的故事既可笑又愚蠢,而后渐渐衍化为成语使用。在古代,钟是一种乐器,随着时代的变迁,钟逐渐被铃取代。于是,"掩耳盗铃"的说法就沿用开来。

The story of Cover the Ears to Steal the Bell **satirizes**③ those **ignorant**④ people who only know how to see things from their own **perspective**⑤ and end up fooling themselves.

掩耳盗铃的故事讽刺了那些愚昧无知的人,他们只知道从自己的角度看待问题,最终只能自欺欺人。

Whether the person who stole the bell covers his ears or not, the bell is an objective existence, which will not go away by man's will. So the behavior of the thief is an extreme **manifestation**⑥ of subjective **idealism**⑦.

无论盗铃人是否捂住耳朵,铃声都是客观存在的,不会根据人的主观意志而消失。因此,盗铃人的行为是一种主观唯心主义的极端表现。

佳句点睛 Punchlines

1. The story of Cover the Ears to Steal the Bell is extremely **ironic**⑧.

掩耳盗铃的故事具有很强的讽刺性。

2. The behavior of the person who stole the bell is an extreme manifestation of subjective idealism.

盗铃人的行为是一种主观唯心主义的极端表现。

3. The foolishness of the person who stole the bell is simply self-deceptive.

盗铃人愚蠢的行为简直是自欺欺人。

情景对话 Situational Dialogue

A: Look at the sentence "The cat closes its eyes when stealing the cream." Who can explain it?

B: I think it's a blind cat.

A: A strange idea. Sit down, please. Anyone else?

C: The cat deceives itself, just likes a man who covers his ears to steal a bell.

A: Good. Go on, please.

C: Once upon the time, a man found a beautiful bell and wanted to carry it off on his back. But it was too heavy for him, so he tried to knock it into pieces with a hammer. However, it sounded very loudly. The thief was so frightened that he covered his ears with his hands immediately, and then the sound became much lower. He thought that in this way nobody could hear its sound clearly.

A: Great! Thank you for telling us this interesting story.

A: 请看这句话:"这只猫在偷奶油时闭上了眼睛。"谁能解释一下这个句子吗?

B: 我想这是一只瞎眼的猫。

A: 这是个很特别的想法。请坐。还有谁能解释一下呢?

C: 这只猫是自己骗自己,就像一个人偷钟时捂住自己的耳朵一样。

A: 很好,请继续讲。

C: 很久以前,有个人发现了一口漂亮的大钟,很想把它背回家。可是钟太沉了,于是他就想用锤子把钟敲碎。而他刚一动手,钟就响了起来。这个人吓得赶紧捂住自己的耳朵,之后钟声渐渐减轻了很多。他以为只要捂住自己的耳朵别人就听不到了。

A: 太棒了!谢谢你告诉我们这么有趣的故事。

生词注解　Notes

① ridiculous /rɪˈdɪkjələs/　*adj.* 荒谬的;荒唐的

② eliminate /ɪˈlɪmɪneɪt/　vt. 清除；消除

③ satirize /ˈsætəraɪz/　vt. 讽刺；讥讽

④ ignorant /ˈɪɡnərənt/　adj. (对某事物)不了解的；无知的

⑤ perspective /pəˈspektɪv/　n. 视角；观点

⑥ manifestation /ˌmænɪfeˈsteɪʃn/　n. 显示；表明

⑦ idealism /aɪˈdiːəlɪzəm/　n. 唯心主义；唯心论

⑧ ironic /aɪˈrɒnɪk/　adj. 讽刺的；反语的

画饼充饥

Draw a Cake to Satisfy Hunger

导入语　Lead-in

　　画饼充饥,出自曹操的孙子曹睿之口。曹睿是三国时代魏国的第二代君王,他有个亲信大臣名叫卢毓。据晋代陈寿的《三国志·魏书·卢毓传》记载:有一次,曹睿想找一位合适的人担任"中书郎"一职,便请卢毓推荐,并且告诉他千万别推荐徒有虚名的人:"选举莫取有名,名如画地作饼,不可啖也。"意思是说,选拔人才不要单凭名声,名声好比画在地上的饼,是没法吃的。后人就从这个故事中提炼出了"画饼充饥"这个成语,比喻用不切实际的空想来满足自己,是难以解决实际问题的。

文化剪影 Cultural Outline

Cao Rui used the **appropriate**① **metaphor**② to hit the nail on the head, bringing people meaningful thinking. Later, many scholars **quoted**③ this story, and Draw a Cake to Satisfy Hunger has gradually become a well-known idiom.

曹睿运用贴切的比喻一语中的，发人深省。后来，许多文人引用这个典故，画饼充饥逐渐成为人们耳熟能详的成语。

The story of Draw a Cake to Satisfy Hunger tells people that it is **absurd**④ to dream of solving problems, and that only those who get down to work down-to-earth are truly **talented**⑤.

画饼充饥的故事告诉人们空想解决问题荒谬可笑，只有脚踏实地做事的人才有真才实学。

In the traditional culture of ancient China, it is an **eternal**⑥ truth that people regard food as their first necessity. Cao Rui, King of Wei, compared people's reputation with his paintings of cakes, showing that the ancient Kings attached great importance to people's **livelihood**⑦ and talents.

在中国古代传统文化中，民以食为天是亘古不变的真理。魏王曹睿以画饼来比喻人的声誉，可见古代帝王对民生和人才的重视。

佳句点睛　Punchlines

1. Those who draw a cake to satisfy hunger are these who aren't down-to-earth.

画饼充饥的人不是脚踏实地的人。

2. It is an eternal truth that people regard food as the first necessity of their life.

民以食为天是亘古不变的真理。

3. Draw a cake to satisfy hunger is just a pipe dream.

画饼充饥不过是一种不切实际的空想。

情景对话　Situational Dialogue

A: Casey, I'll show you a picture.

B: Well, it's just a picture of people and cakes. Anything special?

A: Let me explain it. It's an old story. In the Period of the Three Kingdoms, Cao Rui, King of Wei, wanted to select a capable man to work for him. He said to his minister, "When choosing a talented person, the reputation doesn't mean anything. A false reputation is just like a picture of a cake, so it can't **relieve**[®] hunger."

B: Yeah. It cannot draw a cake to satisfy hunger. That's a perfect metaphor.

A: 凯西,给你看张图。

B: 图上只画了人和饼,有什么特别的吗?

A: 我告诉你吧,这是一个古老的故事。三国时期,魏王曹睿想挑选一位人才为自己效力,他对大臣说:"选拔人才时,名声并不重要。虚假的名声就如同画的饼一样,不能解决肚子饥饿的问题啊!"

B: 对啊,画饼不能充饥。这个比喻再恰当不过了。

生词注解　Notes

① appropriate /əˈprəuprɪət/　*adj.* 合适的;恰当的

② metaphor /ˈmetəfə(r)/　*n.* 暗喻;隐喻

③ quote /kwəut/　*vt.* 引用;引述

④ absurd /əbˈsɜːd/　*adj.* 荒谬的;荒唐的

⑤ talented /ˈtæləntɪd/　*adj.* 有才能的;多才的

⑥ eternal /ɪˈtɜːnl/　*adj.* 永恒的;不朽的

⑦ livelihood /ˈlaɪvlɪhʊd/　*n.* 生计;生活

⑧ relieve /rɪˈliːv/　*vt.* 减轻;缓和

狐假虎威

The Fox Borrows the Tiger's Fierceness

 导入语　Lead-in

　　狐假虎威，源自先秦时代寓言故事《战国策·楚策一》。讲的是战国时期，在楚国最昌盛的时候，北方诸侯国都很害怕楚宣王的大将昭奚恤。宣王百思不得其解，就问身边的大臣。有一位名叫江乙的大臣向他讲了一个有趣的故事：一头凶猛的老虎外出觅食时抓住了一只狐狸，狡猾的狐狸说自己是天帝派来管理百兽的，让老虎跟着它去森林里走一圈看看。果然，百兽见状都狂奔而逃。老虎不明白它们是怕自己才逃走的，还以为是怕狐狸呢。后人从这个故事中引申出了"狐假虎威"这一成语,比喻仰仗或倚仗别人的权势来欺压恐吓、作威作福或招摇撞骗。

文化剪影 Cultural Outline

The tale that the Fox Borrows the Tiger's Fierceness is a household story in China. In order to **facilitate**① writing and memory, the story was gradually **condensed**② into idioms and widely spread.

在中国,狐假虎威是一个家喻户晓的故事。为了便于书写和记忆,这个故事渐渐被浓缩为成语,得到了广泛传播。

The **sly**③ fox used the tiger's power to scare away the wild animals in the forest. The story not only **satirizes**④ those who cheat by others' power, but also those idiots who are used by others and don't know it at all.

狡猾的狐狸借助老虎的威风吓跑了森林里的百兽,这个故事不仅讽刺了那些倚仗别人势力去招摇撞骗的人,也嘲讽了被别人利用而浑然不知的糊涂虫。

The tiger is honored as the "King of Animals" in China. It is a symbol of justice, courage and **majesty**⑤, and the **patron saint**⑥ of the working people. As a result, a variety of tiger cultures have sprung up in China.

老虎在中国被誉为"百兽之王",它是正义、勇猛、威严的象征,是劳动人民喜爱的保护神。因此,各种各样的虎文化在中国层出不穷。

 佳句点睛 Punchlines

1. The cunning fox scared away all the animals in the forest with the power of the tiger.

狡猾的狐狸倚仗老虎的威风吓跑了百兽。

2. In the eyes of Chinese people, fox symbolizes **hypocrisy**[7], **treachery**[8] and cunning.

在中国人看来,狐狸象征着虚伪、奸诈和狡猾。

3. The Chinese believe that the tiger is a symbol of justice, bravery and majesty.

中国人认为老虎是正义、勇猛、威严的象征。

 情景对话 Situational Dialogue

A: How was your day at school?

B: It was great. Mom, I learned an interesting idiom.

A: Can I know the name of it?

B: Sure. The Fox Borrows the Tiger's Fierceness.

A: That sounds nice. Why don't you tell me more about it?

B: OK. One day, when he was hunting for food in the forest, a hungry tiger happened to catch a fox. At this time, the fox suddenly hit upon a good idea to get himself out of the **predicament**⑨. He told the tiger that Heaven sent him to rule over all the animals. But the tiger didn't believe in him. Then the fox suggested both of them walk around the forest. To the tiger's surprise, the animals ran away on seeing them. Sadly, the poor tiger thought they were afraid of the fox, and didn't realize it was his power that scared away all the animals.

A: That's a fantastic story. You're so great!

B: Thank you, mom.

A: 你今天在学校怎么样？

B: 还不错！妈妈，今天我学了一个有趣的成语。

A: 能告诉我是什么吗？

B: 可以啊，是狐假虎威。

A: 听起来很不错！能给我讲一讲吗？

B: 好呀。有一天，一只饥饿的老虎在森林觅食时抓住了一只狐狸。狐狸灵机一动，想到了一个脱身的妙计。它对老虎说自己是天帝派来管理百兽的，老虎不相信。于是，狐狸就让老虎和它一起去森林里走一圈。令老虎惊讶的是，百兽见了它们撒腿就跑。可怜的老虎还以为它们是害怕狐狸呢！根本不知道是自己的威风吓跑了百兽。

A: 这个故事太好了！你真棒！

B: 谢谢妈妈。

生词注解 Notes

① facilitate /fəˈsɪlɪteɪt/　*vt.* 使……容易；促进

② condense /kənˈdens/　*vt.* 使……浓缩；使……压缩

③ sly /slaɪ/　*adj.* 狡猾的；狡黠的

④ satirize /ˈsætəraɪz/　*vt.* 讽刺；讥讽

⑤ majesty /ˈmædʒəstɪ/　*n.* 威严；庄严

⑥ patron saint /ˌpeɪtrən ˈseɪnt/　*n.* 守护神

⑦ hypocrisy /hɪˈpɒkrəsɪ/　*n.* 伪善；虚伪

⑧ treachery /ˈtretʃərɪ/　*n.* 背叛；背信弃义

⑨ predicament /prɪˈdɪkəmənt/　*n.* 困境；窘境

老马识途

An Old Horse Knows the Way

 导入语　Lead-in

老马识途,出自《韩非子·说林上》,讲的是北方少数民族山戎侵犯燕国,燕国派人来齐国求救。齐桓公亲率大军援救燕国。大军凯旋,

但在崇山峻岭的山谷中迷失了方向;足智多谋的相国管仲提议挑出几匹老马,解开缰绳,让它们在大军的最前面带路。最终,他们跟随马匹死里逃生走出了山谷,找到了回齐国的路。"老马识途"这一成语便由此而来,意思是指老马认识路。比喻富有经验的人善于发现规律,能起引导作用。

文化剪影 Cultural Outline

Throughout the history of human civilization, the story that An Old Horse Knows the Way has been quoted by scholars of different times; and through the social development and changes of language habits, it has been developed into a vivid and **concise**① idiom.

纵观人类文明发展史,老马识途的故事一直被不同时代的文人所引用,而后经过社会的发展及语言习惯的变化,演化成为生动简洁的成语。

The story that An Old Horse Knows the Way tells us that experienced people can play a guiding role in dealing with things, and we should be good at using our brains to find the laws of things around us.

老马识途的故事告诉我们,有经验的人在处理事情时可以起到指引的作用,我们做事也要善于动脑,发现周围事物的规律。

The horse's long face and large nasal **cavity**② make it a more developed "**olfactory**③ radar" than other animals, and the horse also has a **keen**④ sense of hearing and can form a strong memory of smell, sound and the way, so it knows the way.

马的脸长且鼻腔大,因此拥有比其他动物更发达的"嗅觉雷达";此外马还拥有灵敏的听觉,对气味、声音以及路途能形成牢固的记忆,因此能够识途。

佳句点睛　Punchlines

1. The story that An Old Horse Knows the Way is still very popular today.

老马识途的故事至今仍脍炙人口。

2. Horses have more developed "olfactory radar's" than other animals.

马拥有比其他动物更为发达的"嗅觉雷达"。

3. Horses have not only a **developed**⑤ sense of smell, but also a keen sense of hearing.

马不仅有发达的嗅觉,还有灵敏的听觉。

情景对话　Situational Dialogue

A: John, how about gonna watch the **equestrian**⑥ event tomorrow?

B: Really? I'd love to. I heard that the horse is a clever animal.

A: Exactly. The old horse knows the way back.

B: How do you know that?

A: I learned that from a book. During the Spring and Autumn Period, the King of Qi led an army to attack a small state in the north in spring. The war didn't come to an end until winter. However, the troops lost their way on the way back. At that time, a minister said that the old horses might know the way back. So he chose several old horses to lead the army. Finally, they found the way home.

B: Oh, that's **incredible**⑦!

A: 约翰,明天一起去看马术比赛怎么样?

B: 真的吗? 我很想去呢! 听说马是一种很聪明的动物。

A: 的确是,老马识途嘛。

B: 你怎么知道的?

A: 我是从一本书上看到的。说的是春秋时期,齐王率军攻打一个北方小国。出征时是春天,战争结束已是冬天了。然而,在归途中大军迷失了方向。这时,一位大臣说也许老马能认识路。于是,他就挑选了几匹老马,让它们走在队伍前面。后来,他们果然找到了回去的路。

B: 哇,真是不可思议啊!

生词注解　Notes

① concise /kənˈsaɪs/　*adj.* 简明的;简洁的

② cavity /ˈkævətɪ/　*n.* 孔;腔

③ olfactory /ɒlˈfæktərɪ/　*adj.* 嗅觉的

④ keen /kiːn/ *adj.* 敏锐的；敏捷的

⑤ developed /dɪˈveləpt/ *adj.* 发达的；成熟的

⑥ equestrian /ɪˈkwestrɪən/ *adj.* 马术的

⑦ incredible /ɪnˈkredəbl/ *adj.* 不能相信的；难以置信的

井底之蛙

A Frog Living at the Bottom of a Well

导入语　Lead-in

　　井底之蛙，源自《庄子·秋水》，说的是一只生活在浅井里的青蛙见到了一只来自东海的大鳖，便兴致勃勃地吹嘘自己独占一井之水，这种快乐谁也比不上。海鳖却告诉青蛙，夏禹时期十年九涝，海水并未增多。商汤时八年七旱，但海水也未减少。大海既不会随时间的长短而改变，也不会因雨量的多少而涨落，这才是生活在东海里最大的快乐！"井底之蛙"这一成语便由此而来，意思是指井底的青蛙认为天只有井口那么大，比喻那些见识短浅、鼠目寸光的人。

文化剪影 Cultural Outline

In the course of Chinese history and culture, the story of the frog living at the bottom of a well and the turtle in the sea has been quoted by many scholars in their own literary works, so it is well known to the public. Later, after a variety of forms of **dissemination**① and development, it has become a well-known idiom.

在中国的历史文化进程中,井底之蛙与大海之鳖的故事被许多文人引用在自己的文学作品之中,因此被大众所熟知。后来,经过多种形式的传播与发展,"井底之蛙"成了妇孺皆知的成语。

The story of A Frog Living at the Bottom of a Well reveals the truth of conducting oneself by a strong contrast. Only those who are knowledgeable will not be blindly **complacent**②.

井底之蛙的故事通过强烈的对比,揭示了做人的道理。只有见多识广、知识渊博的人才不会盲目自满。

Just as the frog at the bottom of a shallow well never knows the vastness of the sea, so the story of the frog in the well reflects, to some extent, the limitations of human **cognitive**③ ability.

浅井之蛙无法得知海之辽阔,该故事在某种程度上也反映了人类认识能力的局限性。

 佳句点睛　Punchlines

1. The story of A Frog Living at the Bottom of a Well tells us that universe has no end and knowledge is infinite.

井底之蛙的故事告诉我们宇宙无终极，学识无穷尽。

2. The **ignorant**④ frog can never realize the happiness of living in the sea.

孤陋寡闻的青蛙永远体会不到生活在海里的快乐。

3. The story of A Frog Living at the Bottom of a Well **satirizes**⑤ those who are short-sighted and blindly complacent.

井底之蛙的故事讽刺了那些见识短浅、盲目自满的人。

 情景对话　Situational Dialogue

A: The summer night in the countryside is so beautiful!

B: Yeah. It's a good time to listen to stories.

A: A good idea! So why don't you tell me one?

B: Okay. Let me think. A long time ago there was a frog living in a well, who was very satisfied with the small world in which it lived. So the frog would **brag**⑥ in public whenever it had a chance. One day, it met a turtle from the sea. Then it told proudly the turtle that living in its small place was the happiest thing in the world. After that, the turtle told it something about the sea, "In ancient times, there were floods nine years out of ten, but the water in the sea didn't rise much. Later there were **droughts**⑦ seven years out of eight, but the water in the sea did not drop much. Only living in the sea can you feel real happiness!"

A: The frog was really so short-sighted.

B: As the saying goes, "We should range far our eye over long **vistas**⑧."

A: 乡村的夏夜真美啊!

B: 是呀。正是听故事的好时候。

A: 好主意!要不你讲一个吧?

B: 好,让我想想。很久以前,有一只青蛙住在一口井里,它对自己生活的小天地满意极了,一有机会就要当众吹嘘一番。有一天,它碰到一只海鳖。于是,青蛙就向海鳖炫耀,说自己生活在一方小天地里简直是世界上最幸福的事了!听完之后,海鳖对它说:"古时候,十年九涝,但海水并没有涨高多少。后来,八年七旱,海水也没有减少多少。只有住在大海里,你才能感受到真正的快乐!"

A: 这真是一只目光短浅的青蛙。

B: 常言道:"风物长宜放眼量。"

生词注解 Notes

① dissemination /dɪˌsemɪˈneɪʃn/ n. 散布；传播（信息、知识等）

② complacent /kəmˈpleɪsnt/ adj. 自满的；自鸣得意的

③ cognitive /ˈkɒɡnətɪv/ adj. 认知的；感知的

④ ignorant /ˈɪɡnərənt/ adj.（对某事物）不了解的；无知的

⑤ satirize /ˈsætəraɪz/ vt. 讽刺；讥讽

⑥ brag /bræɡ/ v. 吹嘘；自吹自擂

⑦ drought /draʊt/ n. 久旱；旱灾

⑧ vista /ˈvɪstə/ n. 远景；前景

守株待兔

Stay by a Stump to Wait for Hares

 导入语　Lead-in

守株待兔，出自《韩非子·五蠹》："宋人有耕者。田中有株，兔走触株，折颈而死。因释其耒而守株，冀复得兔。兔不可复得，而身为宋国笑。今欲以先王之政，治当世之民，皆守株之类也。"说的是宋国有个农夫在田间耕作时，看见一只兔子撞死在树桩上，他毫不费力地捡走了这只兔子。从此，他便丢下农活，守候在树桩边，希望再捡到撞死的兔子。这个农夫再也没有捡到兔子，而他却成了宋国人口中的笑料。"守株待兔"原比喻希望不经过努力就能得到成功的侥幸心理，现在也指固守狭隘经验而不知变通。

 文化剪影　Cultural Outline

The story of Stay by a Stump to Wait for Hares is easy to understand, and it contains a stronger philosophical nature, so it is loved by people. In the process of social development and changes, the story has also been **refined**① into a familiar idiom.

　　守株待兔这个故事通俗易懂,富含较强的哲理性,因而受到人们的喜爱。在社会不断发展与变化的过程中,该故事也被凝练成了大家耳熟能详的成语。

Although the story of Stay by a Stump to Wait for Hares is simple and short, it represents Han Feizi's political thought. He hoped that the rulers would **conform**② to the social development to **adjust**③ the strategy of governing the country instead of being as **pedantic**④ and ridiculous as the person who stayed by the stump to wait for hares.

　　守株待兔的故事虽简短,但却体现了韩非子的政治思想。他希望统治者根据社会的发展去调整治国方略,而不是像守株待兔的人一样迂腐可笑。

The simple story contains **abstract**⑤ truth, which has the artistic effect of being thought-provoking and warning the people. That's just the **unique**⑥ reasoning skills of ancient saints.

　　浅显的故事中蕴含着抽象的道理,具有耐人寻味和警醒世人的艺术效果,这正是古代圣贤独特的说理技巧。

佳句点睛　Punchlines

1. The story of Stay by a Stump to Wait for Hares is **intriguing**⑦.
守株待兔的故事耐人寻味。

2. Han Feizi hoped the rulers would adjust the strategy of governing the country with the social development instead of being as pedantic as the person who stayed by a stump to wait for hares.
韩非子希望统治者根据社会的发展去调整治国方略,而不是像守株待兔的人一样迂腐。

3. The story of Stay by a Stump to Wait for Hares is simple, but contains abstract truth.
守株待兔这个故事虽然浅显,但却蕴含着抽象的道理。

情景对话　Situational Dialogue

A: Jeff, how about hunting on weekends?

B: Well, I don't think it's a good idea. Why not stay by a stump to wait for hares?

A: Are you kidding?

B: No. A farmer who lived in the state of Song saw a hare run into a stump **accidentally**⑧ and die of a broken neck.

A: Then what happened?

B: The farmer took the hare home and cooked a delicious meal for himself. From then on, he stayed by the stump every day to wait for more hares.

A: I bet he couldn't wait for any hare.

B: Yeah. The people in the village laughed at him for taking the accidental for the **inevitable**②.

A：杰夫,周末去打猎怎么样?

B：嗯,我不觉得那是个好主意。你不如守株待兔?

A：你在开玩笑吧?

B：不是。宋国有个农夫就偶然看见一只兔子撞在了树桩上,摔断脖子而死。

A：后来呢?

B：这个农夫就把兔子带回家,美滋滋地吃了一顿兔肉。从此以后,他就天天守在树桩边,等待着兔子的到来。

A：我打赌,他一只兔子也等不到。

B：是啊。村里的人都笑他把偶然当成了必然。

生词注解　Notes

① refine /rɪˈfaɪn/　vt. 改善;使……精练

② conform /kənˈfɔːm/　v. 顺应(大多数人或社会);随潮流

③ adjust /əˈdʒʌst/　vt. 调整;使……适应

④ pedantic /pɪˈdæntɪk/ *adj.* 迂腐的；学究气的

⑤ abstract /ˈæbstrækt/ *adj.* 抽象的；纯理论的

⑥ unique /juˈniːk/ *adj.* 独特的；独一无二的

⑦ intriguing /ɪnˈtriːgɪŋ/ *adj.* 引人入胜的；神秘的

⑧ accidentally /ˌæksɪˈdentəlɪ/ *adv.* 意外地；偶然地

⑨ inevitable /ɪnˈevɪtəbl/ *adj.* 必然的；不可避免的

鹬蚌相争

A Battle Between a Snipe and a Clam

   导入语 Lead-in

鹬蚌相争,出自《战国策·燕策》:"蚌方出曝,而鹬啄其肉,蚌合而箝其喙。鹬曰:'今日不雨,明日不雨,即有死蚌!'蚌亦谓鹬曰:'今日不出,明日不出,即有死鹬!'两者不肯相舍,渔者得而并禽之。"战国时期,当赵国想要攻打燕国时,著名说客苏代为了燕国的利益挺身而出,用"鹬蚌相争"的故事委婉地劝谏赵王审时度势、权衡利弊,从而成功阻止了赵国攻打燕国。这个成语一般与"渔翁得利"连用,是"鹬蚌相争,渔翁得利"的省略语,意思是鹬和蚌争斗对抗,僵持不下,使路过的渔翁捡了便宜。比喻双方相持不下,使第三方从中得利。

文化剪影　Cultural Outline

For thousands of years, the story of A Battle between a **Snipe**① and a **Clam**② has been widely **circulated**③ and quoted by scholars of different times. Until the Xianglingzi in Qing Dynasty used it as an idiom in the article, it has been used ever since.

千百年来,鹬蚌相争的故事一直广为流传,并被不同时期的文人所引用。直到清代的湘灵子在文章中将其作为成语使用后,才一直沿用至今。

Su Dai not only succeeded in persuading the King of Zhao through the story of a Battle between a Snipe and a Clam, but also revealed some truth, leaving room for thinking.

苏代借用鹬蚌相争的故事不仅成功地说服了赵王,而且也揭示了一定的道理,给人留下了思考的余地。

Facing the **ambitious**④ King of Zhao, Su Dai didn't directly state the right or wrong of the matter, but skillfully used a story to **illustrate**⑤ the truth, showing not only his extraordinary courage, but also his superb language art.

面对雄心勃勃的赵王,苏代不是直接陈述事情的对与错,而是巧用故事来阐明道理,既展示了他过人的胆识,又表现了他高超的语言艺术。

佳句点睛　Punchlines

1. The story of A Battle between a Snipe and a Clam has been widely circulated for thousands of years.

千百年来,鹬蚌相争的故事一直广为流传。

2. It is really ingenious that Su Dai used the story of A Battle between a Snipe and a Clam to persuade the King of Zhao.

苏代借用鹬蚌相争的故事来说服赵王,实属巧妙!

3. Su Dai had both extraordinary courage and superb language art.

苏代既有过人的胆识,又有高超的语言艺术。

情景对话　Situational Dialogue

A: Grandpa, I found many clams on the river bank.

B: Well, snipes will be lucky.

A: Why do you say that?

B: In fact, there's an interesting story between them.

A: Why don't you tell me the story?

B: Okay. One day a clam opened its shell to sunbathe on a beach. Suddenly a snipe stuck its **beak**① in the clam. The latter closed its shell immediately, and **trapped**② the snipe's beak. The clam refused to open its shell, and the snipe refused to remove its beak. Neither of them would give in. Finally, a fisherman came along and caught both of them.

A: Wow, the fisherman became a **beneficiary**⑥.

B: Yeah.

A: 爷爷,我发现河边有许多河蚌。

B: 嗯,那鹬鸟就走运了!

A: 您为什么这么说呢?

B: 事实上,它们之间有一个趣事呢。

A: 您给我讲讲呗!

B: 好啊。有一天,一只河蚌张开壳,在沙滩上晒太阳。突然,有只鹬鸟去啄河蚌的肉,河蚌急忙把壳合上,夹住了鹬鸟的嘴。它们俩互不相让,谁也不肯妥协。后来,一个渔翁经过,就把它俩都捉走了。

A: 哇!这渔翁成了受益者。

B: 是呀!

生词注解 Notes

① snipe /snaɪp/   *n.* 沙锥(喙长直,生活在潮湿地区)

② clam /klæm/   *n.* 蚌;蛤蜊

③ circulate /ˈsɜːkjəleɪt/   *v.* 传播;流传

④ ambitious /æmˈbɪʃəs/   *adj.* 有野心的;有雄心的

⑤ illustrate /ˈɪləstreɪt/   *vt.* (用示例、图画等)说明;解释

⑥ beak /biːk/ *n.* 鸟喙；鸟嘴

⑦ trap /træp/ *vt.* 使……落入险境；使……陷入困境

⑧ beneficiary /ˌbenɪˈfɪʃərɪ/ *adj.* 受益人；受惠者

完璧归赵

Return the Jade Intact to the State of Zhao

  导入语 Lead-in

完璧归赵,出自西汉时期司马迁的《史记·廉颇蔺相如列传》。战国时期,秦国看中了赵国的无价之宝和氏璧,打算用十五座城邑换取和氏璧。赵国很为难,担心秦国没有诚意。赵相蔺相如携璧入秦,发现秦王有诈。于是,他凭借大智大勇携璧以死相逼,宁为玉碎,要秦王先划让城邑。秦王理屈,退殿而去,蔺相如连夜将和氏璧送回赵国,史称"完璧归赵"。完璧归赵原指蔺相如将和氏璧完好地自秦国带回赵国,后比喻把原物完好地归还原主。

文化剪影　Cultural Outline

In the long river of splendid Chinese culture, the historical story that Lin Xiangru returned the jade **intact**[1] to the state of Zhao has been praised by people all the time, and it appears in various literary and artistic works. Then "Return the Jade Intact to the State of Zhao" has been handed down as an idiom.

在中国灿烂的文化长河中,蔺相如完璧归赵的历史故事一直被人们传颂着,并出现在各种文学艺术作品中。后来,"完璧归赵"作为成语流传开来。

The story that Lin Xiangru returned the jade intact to the state of Zhao not only shows his courage and wisdom, but reflects his noble **patriotism**[2].

蔺相如完璧归赵的故事不仅体现了他的勇敢和智慧,更表现了他高尚的爱国主义精神。

In Chinese historical **documents**[3] of thousands of years, there are many records and legends about the Jade of the He Family. It is a famous piece of beautiful jade in ancient China, and has been regarded as a priceless **treasure**[4] for thousands of years. However, with the change of the times, the Jade of the He Family has disappeared and become a legendary mystery.

在中国几千年的历史文献中,有许多关于和氏璧的记载和传说。

它是中国古代一块著名的美玉，数千年来被奉为"无价之宝"。随着时代的更迭，和氏璧早已下落不明，成了富有传奇色彩的一个谜。

佳句点睛　Punchlines

1. The historical story that Lin Xiangru returned the jade intact to the state of Zhao is **enduring**⑤ in China.

蔺相如完璧归赵的历史故事在中国经久不衰。

2. As a courageous and **resourceful**⑥ man, Lin Xiangru always put the national interests first.

有勇有谋的蔺相如时刻以自己的国家利益为重。

3. The Jade of the He Family was a national treasure of great symbolic significance and cultural value in Chinese history.

和氏璧是中国历史上一件极具象征意义和文化价值的瑰宝。

情景对话　Situational Dialogue

A: Be quiet, please. I'll show you a picture of Lin Xiangru first. Do you know him?

B: He was a character of *The Records of the Historian*.

A: Yes. Thank you. Anything else? Zhang Yinuo, please.

C: He returned the jade of the He Family to the state of Zhao.

A: Can you explain it?

C: Okay. During the Warring States Period, when learning that the state of Zhao possessed a priceless piece of jade known as "the Jade of the He Family," the King of Qin determined to **acquire**⑦ it. Then he sent a messenger to Zhao, saying that he was willing to offer fifteen of his cities in exchange for the treasure. However, the King of Zhao knew the King of Qin was **crafty**⑧, so he sent Lin Xiangru to Qin with the jade. Finally, Lin Xiangru took back the jade to Zhao with courage and wisdom.

A: Well said!

A: 请保持安静！首先，我给大家看一张蔺相如的图片。你们了解他吗？

B: 他是《史记》中的一个人物。

A: 是的，谢谢你。还有呢？请张一诺来回答。

C: 他把和氏璧送回了赵国。

A: 你能否解释一下呢？

C: 可以。战国时期，秦王听说赵国得到了一件无价之宝和氏璧，打算用十五座城邑换取它。赵王知道秦王狡诈，于是就派蔺相如带着和氏璧前往秦国。最后，蔺相如凭借自己的英勇和智慧，把和氏璧带回了赵国。

A: 说得太好了！

生词注解　Notes

① intact /ɪnˈtækt/　*adj.* 完好无损的；完整的

② patriotism /ˈpætrɪətɪzəm/　*n.* 爱国主义；爱国精神

③ document /ˈdɒkjumənt/　*n.* 文件；公文

④ treasure /ˈtreʒə(r)/　*n.* 财宝；珍品

⑤ enduring /ɪnˈdjʊərɪŋ/　*adj.* 持久的；耐久的

⑥ resourceful /rɪˈsɔːsfl/　*adj.* 足智多谋的；随机应变的

⑦ acquire /əˈkwaɪə(r)/　*vt.* 获得；得到

⑧ crafty /ˈkrɑːftɪ/　*adj.* 狡诈的；诡计多端的

围魏救赵

Besiege the State of Wei to Rescue the State of Zhao

导入语　Lead-in

围魏救赵，出自《史记·孙子吴起列传》，讲的是发生在战国时期的一场经典战役。当时，魏国围攻赵国都城邯郸，赵国向齐国求救。齐国命田忌、孙膑率军救赵，趁魏国都城兵力空虚之际，引兵直攻魏国。魏军回救，齐军乘其疲惫，于中途大败魏军，赵国之围遂解。这种战略后来常为兵家采用，被称为"围魏救赵"。该成语原指齐国通过围攻魏国，迫使魏国撤回攻打赵国的部队，从而使赵国转危为安；后指袭击敌人后方的据点，迫使敌军撤退的战术。

文化剪影 Cultural Outline

The story of **Besiege**① the State of Wei to Rescue the State of Zhao first appeared in *The Records of the Historian* and was later used in *The Romance of the Three Kingdoms* in the form of an idiom by Luo Guanzhong of the Ming Dynasty. Thereupon it has been common in literary works and become a household idiom.

围魏救赵的故事最早出现于《史记》中,后来明朝的罗贯中在《三国演义》中将其以成语的形式使用,之后便常见于文学著作中,成为家喻户晓的成语。

Sun Bin used the strategy of Besiege the State of Wei to Rescue the State of Zhao, which is a very famous example of war in Chinese history, reflecting Sun Bin's wisdom of analyzing problems and making the best use of the situation.

孙膑用围攻魏国的策略来解决赵国的危困,这在中国历史上是一个非常有名的战例,体现了孙膑善于分析问题和因势利导的聪明才智。

Besiege the State of Wei to Rescue the State of Zhao is both an idiom and a **tactic**②, which is a pretty brilliant **ingenuity**③ in the Thirty-Six **Stratagems**④, to solve the problem in a **reverse**⑤ way, so as to get a magical effect.

围魏救赵既是一个成语,又是一种战术,是三十六计中一条相当精彩的智谋，以逆向思维的方式去解决问题，从而得到神奇的效果。

佳句点睛 Punchlines

1. Besiege the State of Wei to Rescue the State of Zhao is both an idiom and a tactic.

围魏救赵既是一个成语又是一种战术。

2. The tactic of Besiege the State of Wei to Rescue the State of Zhao has been **appreciated**^⑥ by militarists of all ages and still has its vitality till now.

围魏救赵的战法为历代军事家所欣赏，至今仍有生命力。

3. Besiege the State of Wei to Rescue the State of Zhao is a pretty brilliant ingenuity in the Thirty-Six Stratagems.

围魏救赵是三十六计中非常精彩的一条智谋。

情景对话 Situational Dialogue

A: Hi, Mr. Li.

B: Hi, Alice. What can I do for you?

A: I'm confused about the idiom of Besiege the State of Wei to Rescue the State of Zhao.

B: It's a historical story that happened in the Warring States Period. The state of Wei attacked the state of Zhao and laid **siege**① to its capital Handan. Zhao turned to Qi for help, so the army of Qi attacked the capital of Wei. On hearing that, the Wei general rushed his army back to defend the capital. However, the troops of Wei were **ambushed**③ and defeated when they retreated in haste. The state of Zhao was thus rescued.

A: It turned out to be a story about the war.

B: Yeah.

A: 李先生,你好!

B: 你好,爱丽丝。有什么事吗?

A: 我没弄明白围魏救赵这个成语。

B: 它是发生在战国时期的一个历史故事。魏国围攻了赵国的都城邯郸。于是,赵国向齐国求救。齐国就命军队围攻了魏国的都城。魏国大将得知都城被围,便急忙回师解救。可是,魏军慌忙撤退之际又中了埋伏,败下阵来。赵国因此得救。

A: 原来它是跟战争有关的故事呀。

B: 是啊。

 生词注解 Notes

① besiege /bɪˈsiːdʒ/ vt. 围困;包围

② tactic /ˈtæktɪk/ n. 战术;兵法

③ ingenuity /ˌɪndʒəˈnjuːətɪ/ n. 足智多谋;心灵手巧

④ stratagem /ˈstrætədʒəm/ *n.* 策略；计谋

⑤ reverse /rɪˈvɜːs/ *adj.* 相反的；颠倒的

⑥ appreciate /əˈpriːʃieɪt/ *vt.* 欣赏；领会

⑦ siege /siːdʒ/ *n.* (军队对城镇的)围困；包围

⑧ ambush /ˈæmbʊʃ/ *vt.* 伏击；埋伏

班门弄斧

Show off One's Skill with an Axe Before Lu Ban

 导入语 Lead-in

　　班门弄斧,源自唐朝柳宗元的《王氏伯仲唱和诗序》:"操斧于班、郢之门,斯强颜耳。"成语中的"班"是指鲁班,他是中国古代著名的能工巧匠。民间历来把鲁班奉为木匠的始祖,因此无人敢在鲁班门前卖弄使用斧子的技术,也就是说,想在行家面前显示自己的本领,这种太不谦虚的可笑行为被称为"鲁班门前弄大爷",简称"班门弄斧"。该成语比喻没有自知之明,在行家面前卖弄本领,不自量力,也可作自谦之词,表示自己不敢在行家面前逞能。

文化剪影 Cultural Outline

In the long history of Chinese culture, the earliest **embryonic**[①] form of the idiom of Show off One's Skill with an Axe before Lu Ban appeared in Liu Zongyuan's article in the Tang Dynasty. After several changes, it was **condensed**[②] into a simple idiom and has been passed down.

在源远流长的中国文化中,班门弄斧最早的雏形出现在唐朝柳宗元的文章里,后来几经演变被浓缩成为简便的成语流传了下来。

The story of Show off One's Skill with an Axe before Lu Ban shows that the Chinese **attach great importance to**[③] the virtue of modesty. One should not be complacent, but should take a humble attitude. Because only modest people can absorb real knowledge and truth.

班门弄斧的故事说明了中国人十分重视谦虚的美德。做人不可有自满之心,而应虚怀若谷,因为谦虚的人才能学到真正的学问和真理。

Lu Ban was an **outstanding**[④] inventor in ancient China and the forefather of wood **craftsman**[⑤]. For thousands of years, his name and stories have been popular among the masses of the people.

鲁班是中国古代一位出色的发明家,也是木匠的开山鼻祖。几千年来,他的名字和有关他的故事一直在人民群众中广为流传。

佳句点睛 Punchlines

1. Lu Ban was a famous craftsman in ancient times.

鲁班是古代著名的能工巧匠。

2. Lu Ban was not only an outstanding inventor, but also the founder of carpenter.

鲁班既是一位出色的发明家,又是木匠的开山鼻祖。

3. Today, Lu Ban's name has become a **synonym**⑥ for insiders.

如今,鲁班的名字已成为内行人的代称。

情景对话 Situational Dialogue

A: Molly, look at the lifelike statue. Do you know who it is?

B: Er, sorry, Nana. Could you tell me who it is?

A: It's Lu Ban, a **consummate**⑦ carpenter in ancient times.

B: Had he achieved anything?

A: Well, he had a lot of achievements in his life. Carpenters respect him as the **originator**⑧. It's said that he carved a colorful wooden phoenix that kept flying in the sky for three days.

B: It sounds like he was an expert.

A: Of course. There's an idiom of Show off One's Skill with an

Axe before Lu Ban, which means those who show off their slight **accomplishment**④ in front of experts.

B: Thank you, Nana. This is the first idiom I have learned since I came to China.

A: My pleasure.

A: 莫莉，看这尊栩栩如生的塑像，你知道这是谁吗？

B: 呃，不好意思，娜娜。你能告诉我吗？

A: 这是鲁班，他是古代一位技术高超的木匠。

B: 他有什么成就吗？

A: 嗯，他一生中有很多成就，木匠们都奉他为祖师。据说他曾用木头做了一只五彩斑斓的凤凰，能够在空中飞翔三天不掉下来。

B: 听起来他是个行家。

A: 当然了！有一个成语叫班门弄斧，意思是说在行家面前卖弄自己微不足道的本领。

B: 谢谢你，娜娜。这是我来中国后学到的第一个成语。

A: 不客气。

生词注解 Notes

① embryonic /ˌembrɪˈɒnɪk/ *adj.* 胚胎的；萌芽期的

② condense /kənˈdens/ *vt.* 使……浓缩；使……压缩

③ attach /əˈtætʃ/ great importance to 重视

④ outstanding /aʊtˈstændɪŋ/ *adj.* 优秀的；杰出的；出色的

⑤ craftsman /ˈkrɑːftsmən/ n. 工匠；手艺人

⑥ synonym /ˈsɪnənɪm/ n. 同义词；同义字

⑦ consummate /kənˈsʌmət/ adj. 技艺高超的；完美的

⑧ originator /əˈrɪdʒɪneɪtə(r)/ n. 创始人；发起者

⑨ accomplishment /əˈkʌmplɪʃmənt/ n. 成就；成绩

兔死狗烹

Kill the Hounds for Food Once the Hares Are Bagged

 **Lead-in**

兔死狗烹，源自司马迁的《史记·越王勾践世家》。范蠡是春秋时期越王勾践的一位重要谋臣，他和文种为勾践灭掉吴国、称霸中原立下了汗马功劳。范蠡功成身退，并用"狡兔死，走狗烹"的道理劝文种隐退，但文种没有听从，后来被勾践猜忌而赐死。"兔死狗烹"便由此引申而来。意思是兔子死尽了，就会烹食捉兔子的猎狗。比喻事成之后过河拆桥，抛弃或杀掉有功之人。与之相近的还有：鸟尽弓藏，得鱼忘筌。

文化剪影　Cultural Outline

With the continuous development of society and language, the story of Kill the **Hounds**① for Food Once the Hares Are **Bagged**② has gradually been **refined**③ into a simple idiom, which is widely spread, carried forward and applied to social life.

随着社会和语言的不断发展,"狡兔死,走狗烹"的故事渐渐被精炼为成语使用,从而得到了广泛的传播和发扬,应用到了社会生活当中。

The story of Kill the Hounds for Food Once the Hares Are Bagged not only shows the **autocratic**④ power of the ruling class, but also is a kind of advice for future generations by the ancients. Such tragic stories have made the Chinese sigh and **lament**⑤ for thousands of years.

兔死狗烹的故事不仅表现了统治阶级的独裁专权,也是古人对后人的一种忠告。这样的悲剧故事数千年来让中国人扼腕叹息。

The culture of **seclusion**⑥ is an important part of traditional Chinese culture. Fan Li chose to retire from the world after his success, which was a way for the ancient person to **preserve**⑦ himself and a philosophy of life.

隐居文化是中国传统文化中重要的一部分。范蠡选择功成后隐居避世,这是古人保护自身的一种方式,更是一种处世之道。

佳句点睛 Punchlines

1. The story of Kill the Hounds for Food Once the Hares Are Bagged is not only Fan Li's advice to Wen Zhong, but the ancient people's to future generations.

"狡兔死,走狗烹"不仅是范蠡对文种的忠告,也是古人对后人的忠告。

2. The story of Kill the Hounds for Food Once the Hares Are Bagged has made the Chinese sigh and lament for thousands of years.

兔死狗烹的故事让中国人扼腕叹息了几千年。

3. Seclusion was a way for the ancients to protect themselves and a philosophy of life.

隐居是古人保护自身的一种方式,也是一种处世之道。

情景对话 Situational Dialogue

A: Excuse me, Su Meng. What book are you reading?

B: Oh, *The Records of the Historian*.

A: Is it very interesting? I found you have been reading it.

B: Yes, there are many interesting stories in it. By the way, do you know Fan Li?

A: No. Any stories about Fan Li?

B: Sure. Fan Li was a talented person, he and Wen Zhong did great **contribution**⑧ to the state of Yue. However, Fan Li decided to live in seclusion when the state of Yue became strong. Later, he wrote to Wen Zhong in the letter, "Once the hares are bagged, the hounds will be killed for food." But Wen Zhong didn't take the advice. Finally the king of Yue believed the **slanderous**⑨ gossip and ordered Wen Zhong to kill himself.

A: It is a sad story. But the sentence Fan Li wrote in the letter is profound.

B: Yeah. Later it has evolved into an idiom.

A: 打扰一下,苏萌。你在看什么书？

B: 噢,《史记》。

A: 这本书很有趣吗？我见你最近一直在读它。

B: 是呀,书里有许多有意思的故事。顺便问一下,你知道范蠡吗？

A: 不知道。有什么跟范蠡有关的故事吗？

B: 当然有了！范蠡是一个才华横溢的人,他和文种一起为越国做出了巨大贡献。可是,当越国强大之后,范蠡却选择了隐居。后来,他写信给文种:"狡兔死,走狗烹。"文种却没有采纳他的建议。最后,越王听信了谗言,赐文种自尽。

A: 这是一个悲伤的故事。不过,范蠡在信里说的那句话倒是意味深长。

B: 是的。那句话后来演变成了一个成语。

生词注解 Notes

① hound /haʊnd/   *n.* 猎犬;猎狗

② bag /bæg/   *vt.* 捕获;猎杀(动物)

③ refine /rɪˈfaɪn/   *vt.* 改进;使……精练

④ autocratic /ˌɔːtəˈkrætɪk/   *adj.* 独裁的;专制的

⑤ lament /ləˈment/   *v.* 对……感到悲痛;痛惜

⑥ seclusion /sɪˈkluːʒn/   *n.* 隐居;与世隔绝

⑦ preserve /prɪˈzɜːv/   *vt.* 使……继续存活;保全

⑧ contribution /ˌkɒntrɪˈbjuːʃn/   *n.* 贡献;奉献

⑨ slanderous /ˈslɑːndərəs/   *adj.* 诽谤的;中伤的

望梅止渴

Quench Thirst by Thinking of Plums

 导入语　Lead-in

　　望梅止渴,出自南朝刘义庆《世说新语·假谲》:"魏武行役,失汲道,军皆渴,乃令曰:'前有大梅林,饶子,甘酸,可以解渴。'士卒闻之,口皆出水。乘此得及前源。"说的是魏武帝曹操行军途中,天气炎热似火,军队找不到水源;士兵们都口渴难耐,行军速度十分缓慢。曹操担心贻误战机,心生一计,传令道:"前面有大片梅林,结了很多果子,又酸又甜,可以解渴!"士兵们听后精神为之一振,行军速度快了许多。"望梅止渴"是指梅子酸,人想吃梅子就会流口水,因而止渴。后来比喻愿望无法实现,用空想安慰自己或他人。

 文化剪影 Cultural Outline

In the tide of the times, the form of **Quench**① Thirst by Thinking of Plums has changed unconsciously. It has gradually been **evolved**② from the original simple story into an idiom, and accepted by people and spread on a large scale.

在时代的浪潮中,望梅止渴的形式已经不知不觉地发生了变化。它由最初的简单故事逐渐演变成为成语,并被人们接受,得以大规模流传。

Cao Cao mentioned sweet and sour plums to relieve the solders' thirst when the army had no water, which shows that he was a thoughtful and **flexible**③ man.

曹操在大军无水源的危机情况下,提及酸甜的梅子,以解战士们的口渴之苦,表现了曹操是一个善于思考、懂得变通的人。

Plums contain natural organic acid and has strong sour taste, which can **promote**④ saliva secretion. Cao Cao used people's conditioned **reflex**⑤ towards plums to **boost**⑥ the morale.

梅子含天然有机酸,具有强烈的酸味,可以促进唾液分泌。曹操正是利用人们对梅子的条件反射心理鼓舞了士气。

佳句点睛 Punchlines

1. The story of Quench Thirst by Thinking of Plums reflects Cao Cao's intelligence and wisdom.

望梅止渴的故事体现了曹操的聪明才智。

2. The idiom of Quench Thirst by Thinking of Plums means to comfort oneself with **fantasy**⑦.

望梅止渴的意思是比喻用空想安慰自己或他人。

3. Cao Cao skillfully used people's conditioned reflex towards plums and successfully boosted morale.

曹操巧妙地利用人们对梅子的条件反射心理,成功地鼓舞了士气。

情景对话 Situational Dialogue

A: Nana, how I wish to travel around the world! But I have no money.

B: Well, you can quench thirst by thinking of plums.

A: What's the meaning of that?

B: It's an old idiom about Cao Cao, who was an outstanding figure of Chinese history. One day, his troops marched under the blazing sun in a mountainous area. The journey was long and the sun was **scorch-ing**①, and the soldiers were exhausted and thirsty. At this time Cao Cao ordered his troops to march to the nearby plum trees for a rest and announced that the soldiers would be allowed to eat the juicy sour fruit as much as they desired. At the thought of the fruit, the soldiers felt as if they were actually eating the plums, then they quickened their steps **automatically**②.

A: Oh, I see. Maybe I can travel around the world with fantasy now.

B: Yes, you can have a try.

A: 娜娜,我真希望能周游世界啊！可我没钱。

B: 嗯,你可以望梅止渴呀。

A: 什么意思?

B: 这是一个跟曹操有关的古老成语。曹操是中国历史上一位杰出的人物。有一天,他的部队在山区行军,由于长途跋涉、天气炎热,因此士兵们疲惫不堪、口干舌燥。这时,曹操下令道："前面有大片梅林,大家可以到那里休息并尽情享用酸甜的梅子。"士兵们一听,仿佛梅子已经吃到嘴里,不由得加快了步伐。

A: 噢,我明白了。也许我现在可以想象着周游世界。

B: 是的,你可以试一试。

生词注解 Notes

① quench /kwentʃ/ *n.* 解(渴);止(渴)

② evolve /ɪˈvɒlv/ *vi.* 进化;演变

③ flexible /ˈfleksəbl/ *adj.* 灵活的;柔韧的

④ promote /prəˈməʊt/ *vt.* 促进;推动

⑤ reflex /ˈriːfleks/ *n.* 反射作用;本能反应

⑥ boost /buːst/ *vt.* 使……增长;使……兴旺

⑦ fantasy /ˈfæntəsɪ/ *n.* 幻想;想象

⑧ scorching /ˈskɔːtʃɪŋ/ *adj.* 酷热的

⑨ automatically /ˌɔːtəˈmætɪklɪ/ *adv.* 自动地;无意识地

买椟还珠

Get the Casket and Return the Pearl

 Lead-in

买椟还珠,出自战国时期韩非子的《韩非子·外储说左上》:"楚人有卖其珠于郑者,为木兰之柜,薰以桂椒,缀以珠玉,饰以玫瑰,辑以羽翠。郑人买其椟而还其珠。此可谓善卖椟矣,未可谓善鬻珠也。"说的是有一天,楚王对田鸠说,墨子之学很好,但文词却不美妙,是什么原因呢?田鸠讲了两个故事,其中一个就是:有一个楚国人到郑国去卖珍珠,他用木兰木做了一个装珍珠的盒子,用各种香料和翡翠来装饰它。结果郑国人买了他的盒子,却将珍珠退还。也就是说,那个珠宝商人很善于卖盒子,但不善于卖珍珠啊!后来韩非子说的楚人卖珠的故事被

浓缩成了"买椟还珠"这个成语,用来比喻取舍不当、舍本逐末。

文化剪影　Cultural Outline

Get the Casket and Return the Pearl is a classic idiom that has been around for thousands of years and is well-known to people. For thousands of years it has been **circulated**①, its meaning has changed **fundamentally**.② The interpretation has been used for many years and has become a custom.

买椟还珠是一个流传数千年、人尽皆知的经典成语,经过数千年的流传,其意思已经发生了根本性的变化。其释义多年来沿用至今,早已约定俗成了。

The story of Get the Casket and Return the Pearl makes people understand that too luxuriant **decoration**③ usually **supersedes**④ what really counts. Looking at things cannot focus on form but ignore content and cannot look at the appearance but ignore **essence**⑤.

买椟还珠的故事使人们明白过于华丽的装饰往往会喧宾夺主。看待事物不能只重形式而忽视内容;不能只看外表而忽略本质。

Han Feizi skillfully used fables in the article to explain the reason, vividly reflecting his profound understanding of society and life. Because of the rich **connotation**⑥ and the vivid story, Get the Casket and Return the Pearl has become a well-known idiom and widely been used by people.

韩非子在文章中巧妙地运用寓言故事来说理,形象地体现了他对社会与人生的深刻认识。买椟还珠因其丰富的内涵与生动的故事成为脍炙人口的成语,被人们广泛使用。

佳句点睛　Punchlines

1. Get the Casket and Return the Pearl is a classic idiom that has been around for thousands of years.

买椟还珠是一个流传了数千年的经典成语。

2. Too luxuriant decoration usually supersedes what really **counts**⑦.

过于华丽的装饰往往会喧宾夺主。

3. The jeweler is good at selling the casket but not jewelry.

那个珠宝商善于卖盒子,却不善于卖珠宝。

情景对话　Situational Dialogue

A: Wow, look at the beautiful cover of this book. I wanna take it.

B: Let me see. Well, I don't think the book will help you. It's for children.

A: Yeah. But I really love its cover.

B: Have you ever heard of the story of getting the casket and returning the pearl?

A: Does it have anything to do with buying a book?

B: Sure. A man wanted to sell a precious pearl, and he made a casket for the pearl out of the wood from a **magnolia**② tree, which he **fumigated**⑤ with spices. He even decorated the casket with jade, ornamented it with red gems. Another man bought the casket but gave him back the pearl.

A: What a funny story it is! Okay, I got you.

A: 哇,这本书的封面好漂亮啊!我想买。

B: 让我看看。嗯,我觉得这本书对你无助,它适合小孩子看。

A: 是呀。可我真的好喜欢它的封面。

B: 你听过买椟还珠的故事吗?

A: 这跟买书有什么关系吗?

B: 当然有了!有个人想卖珍珠,他用木兰木为珍珠做了匣子,用香料把匣子熏香,还用翡翠和红宝石加以装饰。另一个人买走了这个匣子,却把珍珠退还给了他。

A: 真是个有趣的故事!好了,我明白你的意思了。

生词注解　Notes

① circulate /ˈsɜːkjəleɪt/　*v.* 传播;流传

② fundamentally /ˌfʌndəˈmentəli/　*adv.* 根本上;完全地

③ decoration /ˌdekəˈreɪʃn/　*n.* 装饰品

④ supersede /ˌsuːpəˈsiːd/　*vt.* 取代;替代(已非最佳选择或已过

时的事物)

⑤ essence /'esns/ *n.* 本质；实质

⑥ connotation /ˌkɒnəˈteɪʃn/ *n.* 含义；隐含意义

⑦ count /kaʊnt/ *v.* 重要；把……算入

⑧ magnolia /mæɡˈnəʊliə/ *n.* 木兰；木兰树

⑨ fumigate /ˈfjuːmɪɡeɪt/ *vt.* 烟熏；熏蒸(以灭虫或消毒)

洛阳纸贵

Paper Is Dear in Luoyang

导入语 Lead-in

洛阳纸贵,出自《晋书·文苑·左思传》:"于是豪贵之家竞相传写,洛阳为之纸贵。"讲的是西晋太康年间一位鼎鼎有名的文学家左思,他的佳作《三都赋》在京城洛阳受到当时名士的广泛赞誉。所以,他的作品一问世,人们就竞相传抄,一时间洛阳的纸张供不应求,价格飙升。"洛阳纸贵"的说法便由此流行开来。"洛阳纸贵"原指洛阳的纸一时供不应求,现在比喻佳作风行一时,广为流传。

 文化剪影 Cultural Outline

In the long course of history, the expression that Paper Is Dear in Luoyang has been widely **circulated**①, which has been **constantly**② developed in people's **quotations**③ and often used by people from generation to generation.

在漫长的历史进程中,洛阳纸贵这个成语经过广泛流传,在引用中不断发展,并被人们世世代代引用。

The story that Paper Is Dear in Luoyang not only shows the power of words, but also reflects the **glorious**④ culture of ancient China to a certain extent.

洛阳纸贵的故事不仅体现了文字传播的力量,也在一定程度上反映出中国古代光辉灿烂的文化。

As the origin of the idiom story that Paper Is Dear in Luoyang, which is a well-known national historical and cultural city and one of the **cradles**⑤ of Chinese **civilization**⑥, with profound historical and cultural **background**⑦.

作为成语故事洛阳纸贵的始发地,洛阳是国家历史文化名城,也是中华文明的发源地之一,具有深厚的历史文化底蕴。

佳句点睛　Punchlines

1. The idiom that Paper Is Dear in Luoyang describes the works as valuable and widely circulated.

洛阳纸贵这个成语形容作品有价值,并广为流传。

2. The idiom that Paper Is Dear in Luoyang reflects the glorious culture of ancient China.

洛阳纸贵这个成语反映出中国古代光辉灿烂的文化。

3. Luoyang is not only a famous historical and cultural city, but also one of the cradles of Chinese civilization.

洛阳不仅是历史文化名城,也是中华文明的发源地之一。

情景对话　Situational Dialogue

A: Kevin, this is my good friend Li Li, who comes from Luoyang.

B: Nice to meet you, Li Li.

C: Nice to meet you too, Kevin.

B: Luoyang is famous for peonies.

C: Yes. Have you been to Luoyang?

B: No. But I love its history.

C: Yeah. It's an ancient city with a long history.

B: I know an idiom known as Paper Is Dear in Luoyang. What does it mean? Is the paper so costly in Luoyang?

C: Of course not. In the Jin Dynasty, there was a famous writer named Zuo Si, whose literary masterpiece *Ode to the Three Capitals* was well received by a mass of readers after it made its appearance to the public. As the art of printing had not been invented at that time, so many people **vied**① with each other in making handwritten copies. The supply of paper fell short of the demand in Luoyang, and then its price went up greatly.

B: That is to say, the idiom means the **overwhelming**② popularity of a new work caused the price of paper to rocket.

C: Right. That's it.

A: 凯文，这是我的好朋友李莉，她来自洛阳。

B: 很高兴见到你，李莉。

C: 我也是，凯文。

B: 洛阳的牡丹很出名。

C: 是的。你去过洛阳吗？

B: 没有。不过，我喜欢洛阳的历史。

C: 嗯，那是一座历史悠久的古老城市。

B: 我知道一个成语叫洛阳纸贵，它是什么意思？是不是说洛阳的纸很贵？

C: 当然不是。说的是晋朝时期有一位著名的文学家左思，他的佳作《三都赋》一经问世，就受到人们的好评。当时还没有发明印刷术,人们只能竞相抄阅,所以洛阳的纸张供不应求,纸价就大幅度上涨了。

B: 也就是说,这个成语的意思是风行一时的作品使纸张的价格上涨了。

C: 对,就是这个意思。

生词注解　Notes

① circulate /ˈsɜːkjəleɪt/　vt. 传播;流传

② constantly /ˈkɒnstəntlɪ/　adv. 始终;一直

③ quotation /kwəʊˈteɪʃn/　n. 引用;引述

④ glorious /ˈɡlɔːrɪəs/　adj. 壮丽的;辉煌的

⑤ cradle /ˈkreɪdl/　n. 策源地;发源地

⑥ civilization /ˌsɪvəlaɪˈzeɪʃn/　n. 文明

⑦ background /ˈbækɡraʊnd/　n.(事态发展等的)背景

⑧ vie /vaɪ/　v. 激烈竞争;争夺

⑨ overwhelming /ˌəʊvəˈwelmɪŋ/　adj. 压倒性的;巨大的